It Was The Only
Her Mind Off Antonio.

Work twenty-four hours a day.

When she was at home, she imagined him there with her. When she slept, he haunted her dreams, making love to her and speaking to her in that beautiful Italian voice of his. When she worked out in the gym, she heard his footfalls on the treadmill next to hers.

He was haunting her. Damn him.

As if she conjured him, he called her. "Nathalie, why haven't you returned my calls?" he asked.

"I'm not sure. I've been busy." Excuses. She knew better than that. "I guess I wanted a chance to get you out of my head."

"Did it work?"

No, she had to admit. *Not at all.*

Dear Reader,

The idea for this book came from an article I read in *Newsweek* about the most expensive luxury car in the world: the Bugatti Veyron. This car is not only superfast and overpriced, it is also very hard to obtain. They make only a limited number, so having one is for an exclusive few.

When I started researching the reason the car was called the Veyron, I found that it was named after an F1 driver, and the story for Antonio, Marco and Dominic fell out of that. Once I started thinking about a car company whose focus was driven by drivers, I knew what I wanted to write.

In *The Moretti Seduction,* Antonio has to try to get the rights back to one of the famous Moretti F1 drivers, Pierre-Henri Vallerio, a man who was once Lorenzo Moretti's best friend. But when Lorenzo married and then divorced Pierre-Henri's daughter, Anna, the two men became enemies. And Pierre-Henri took back the rights to his name being used on the Morettis' number one production car, the Vallerio Roadster.

Antonio is the second Moretti brother to choose between love and the curse that he's grown up under. For Antonio, a playboy and a man used to winning, falling in love doesn't sound threatening. But once he meets and starts to fall for Nathalie Vallerio, all bets are off.

Happy reading!

Katherine

KATHERINE GARBERA

THE MORETTI SEDUCTION

Silhouette® *Desire*

Published by Silhouette Books

America's Publisher of Contemporary Romance

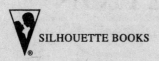 SILHOUETTE BOOKS

ISBN-13: 978-0-373-76935-3
ISBN-10:   0-373-76935-0

Recycling programs
for this product may
not exist in your area.

THE MORETTI SEDUCTION

Books by Katherine Garbera

Silhouette Desire

The Bachelor Next Door #1104
Miranda's Outlaw #1169
Her Baby's Father #1289
Overnight Cinderella #1348
Baby at His Door #1367
Some Kind of Incredible #1395
The Tycoon's Temptation #1414
The Tycoon's Lady #1464
*Cinderella's Convenient
   Husband* #1466
Tycoon for Auction #1504
Cinderella's Millionaire #1520
††*In Bed with Beauty* #1535
††*Cinderella's Christmas
   Affair* #1546
††*Let It Ride* #1558
Sin City Wedding #1567
††*Mistress Minded* #1587
††*Rock Me All Night* #1672
†*His Wedding-Night Wager* #1708
†*Her High-Stakes Affair* #1714

†*Their Million-Dollar Night* #1720
The Once-A-Mistress Wife #1749
***Make-Believe Mistress* #1798
***Six-Month Mistress* #1802
***High-Society Mistress* #1808
**The Greek Tycoon's Secret
   Heir* #1845
**The Wealthy Frenchman's
   Proposition* #1851
**The Spanish Aristocrat's
   Woman* #1858
Baby Business #1888
§*The Moretti Heir* #1927
§*The Moretti Seduction* #1935

††King of Hearts
†What Happens in Vegas…
**The Mistresses
*Sons of Privilege
§Moretti's Legacy

KATHERINE GARBERA

is a strong believer in happily ever after. She's written more than thirty-five books and has been nominated for *Romantic Times BOOKreviews'* career achievement Awards in Series Fantasy and Series Adventure. Her books have appeared on the Waldenbooks/Borders bestseller list for series romance and on the *USA TODAY* extended bestsellers list. Visit Katherine on the Web at www.katherinegarbera.com.

To my daughter...awesomeness in human form.
I am always amazed at the woman you are becoming.
You are smart, funny, pretty and I love you very much.

One

The corporate offices of Moretti Motors were lush and exquisite, combining the best of Italian architecture with the cutting edge of modern design. No expense was spared in the five-story office building in Milan or in the state-of-the-art factory next door where the fastest and priciest production car in the world would soon start rolling off the line.

The only problem was a little sticking point with the name of the car. The Moretti Motors engineering team had reenvisioned the classic and most-talked-about model they had ever made—a 1969 sport roadster that had taken the sports car world by storm and made Lorenzo Moretti a billionaire. Now forty years later they were reintroducing the world to the Vallerio—the car named after the second Formula 1 driver to race for Moretti Motors.

The rights to the name were in question, something that Dominic, Antonio and Marco—the current generation of Morettis—hadn't realized until they had sent out a press release announcing their new car and gotten a cease-and-desist order from Vallerio Inc.

Pierre-Henri Vallerio had started the company after leaving Moretti Motors. Pierre-Henri had been a genius with engine design, and Vallerio Inc. was still at the forefront of that industry today. So it seemed to Antonio that they should be excited to have their name on the tongues of car aficionados everywhere.

The only problem was, as with everything that Antonio's grandfather Lorenzo touched, he'd somehow managed to piss off the Vallerio family.

"Do you ever wonder if *Nono* just had no mojo when it came to women?" Antonio asked his older brother, Dominic.

Dominic was the head of Moretti Motors operations. His title was CEO but he'd always been bossy even when they had been kids.

"The thought has crossed my mind a time or two.

Regardless of what his problem was, he left us a mess to inherit, didn't he?"

"You like the challenge of unraveling his messes," Antonio said. Dom was one of those men who lived for work. Bringing Moretti Motors back to the forefront of the auto world wasn't an easy thing to do. But a challenge like this latest wrinkle with the Vallerio family wouldn't ruffle his older brother. Nor him.

"We need the Vallerio family on board—yesterday."

"I know. It would have been much easier to handle it if we had realized that the rights to the name reverted to them. I mean, who would have signed a contract that said after twenty years of no production car we lost those rights?" Antonio asked.

"Papa," Dominic said.

Their father was a wonderful man and the best father in the world, but when it came to business, Giovanni Moretti just didn't care. Which was why he and his brothers had grown up the poorer relations of the Moretti family.

"Well, I have a meeting scheduled with the attorney." Antonio closed the file folder. The family's attorney was the older daughter, Nathalie Vallerio. From her corporate photo he'd sensed a keen intelligence, as well as an innate beauty that reflected her family's French heritage.

"Good," Dom said. "With Marco falling for Virginia, I'm afraid that our luck may be changing. I don't want to let anything compromise the new production car."

Antonio didn't know if his brother's falling in love with the granddaughter of the woman who'd originally cursed the family was going to change their luck or not. Antonio had never put much stock in luck.

The curse had been put on their grandfather by his onetime lover Cassia Festa. Lorenzo had spurned her love and Cassia, being a Strega—an Italian witch—had gone home and spent days getting angrier and angrier at Lorenzo. When Lorenzo decided to marry Pierre-Henri Vallerio's sister, Cassia had come back to Milan and put a curse on Lorenzo. The words of the curse had been written in her diary, and Virginia, Cassia's granddaughter, had figured out a way to break the curse. Antonio recalled the curse. No Moretti male would ever be lucky in business *and* lucky in love.

Antonio's father had no head for business—hence this mess with Vallerio Inc. But Gio had fallen in love with Philomena and those two had found a deep love and happiness in their life.

He and his brothers had grown up realizing they could be either wealthy or happy in love. Being practical boys, they had taken an oath long ago not to mess things up the way their grandfather had. That meant that they would be lucky in business and not risk falling in love and losing everything they worked to build.

Antonio had found that determination and drive covered what luck didn't. That and his refusal to accept defeat. His entire life he'd never lost at anything once he put his mind to it. And he certainly wasn't about to let Nathalie Vallerio win this battle.

"No problem. The Vallerio family will sign our agreement and I'll bring you back the contract."

Dom rubbed the back of his neck. "I don't need to tell you this, but I won't feel right unless I say it."

Dom rarely worried about the effect of his words, so Antonio raised one eyebrow at him in question. Whatever was on his brother's mind must be something outside the bounds of morality or business ethics. Though at times they'd considered doing things that were in that shadowy gray area, they never had.

Antonio believed that with his determination, Marco's racing talent and Dom's drive, the Moretti brothers didn't need to do anything shady.

"Are you still worried about the corporate espionage?" he asked his brother. They had first realized there was a leak of proprietary information last year at the start of the Grand Prix season. Somehow their main rivals, ESP Motors, had announced an engine intake that was exactly the same as the one that Moretti Motors had been working on for the previous six months.

"I think we can find our leak without doing anything illegal," Antonio said.

"Tony! I'm not going to ask you to do anything illegal. I have got a lead on our corporate spy."

"Then what were you going to ask me?"

Dom leaned over his desk, both arms resting on the dark walnut finish. "Use any means necessary, Tony. If you have to seduce her, then do it. Women like romance."

"Comments like that are the reason why you are single."

Dom made a rude hand gesture, but Tony just laughed. His brother was a great businessman and a natural leader, but when it came to women, Dom didn't trust them and he treated them like disposable commodities. Tony knew that was because of Liza, the woman whom Dom had loved and lost.

There was a knock on the door and Dom bade the person to enter. It was his secretary, Angelina de Luca.

"Sorry to interrupt, Signore Moretti, but the Valerio family is here for Signore Antonio."

"*Grazie,* Angelina. Please direct them to the conference room and get them some refreshments."

Angelina nodded and left the room. Dom watched his secretary leave and Tony wondered to himself if his big brother wasn't as immune to women as he appeared to be.

"You know, with Marco's engagement to Virginia, it might not be a change in our business luck, only our love luck."

Dom shook his head. "For you maybe but not me. I think I have *Nono*'s bad woman mojo."

Tony laughed and stood, clapping his brother on the back.

"I don't have that mojo. And Ms. Nathalie Vallerio," Tony said, looking back down at her photo in the folder, "isn't going to know what hit her."

"*Buon!*"

Nathalie Vallerio had heard all about the Moretti family. Her earliest memories were of her grandfather and father plotting to bring down Lorenzo Moretti. The man was a legendary race car driver who was one of only four drivers to win the Grand Prix championship numerous times. The only person to win more championships was another Moretti. Marco.

And now she was sitting in the lion's den. Back in the one place her grandfather had vowed that no Vallerio would ever stand again. For being her personal hell, the boardroom was quite comfortable.

There was a trophy case at the end of the room with all the Formula 1 racing trophies won by the Moretti drivers, including the ones her grandfather had earned.

On another wall hung photos of the Moretti drivers and of their production cars. They were all good-looking men who had an air about them that seemed to say life was one big adventure. Her grandfather, Pierre-Henri, had always taken great pride that the bestselling production car had borne his name. And of course when Lorenzo broke Nathalie's great-aunt's heart and caused her to die early of heartbreak, Pierre-Henri had done everything in his power to see that Lorenzo no longer had use of the Vallerio name.

Lorenzo's son Giovanni had let the rights to the name lapse in the late '80s and since then Moretti Motors had floundered. But recently under the helm of Dominic, Antonio and Marco the company had resurged and was once again on the verge of taking the car world by storm.

Something that Nathalie was here to make certain they did without involving her family or their name.

She paced around the room, well aware that Antonio was keeping her waiting. Their appointment was supposed to have begun five minutes ago.

One of her pet peeves was tardiness. Disrespect

was the only reason Antonio was keeping her waiting and she would make sure he understood that she wasn't someone to toy with.

"*Ciao,* Signorina Vallerio. I am sorry to have kept you waiting."

She turned to see Antonio Moretti striding toward her. With dark curly hair and classic Roman features, he was quite striking. But that wasn't what held her attention. It was the intelligence and humor she saw in his obsidian eyes. This was a man who made her catch her breath—and that wasn't like her.

She lifted her hand to shake his and then realized that she'd been doing business with Americans for too long. She'd forgotten that Italians always greeted with a kiss on the cheek.

Antonio took her hand and pulled her close. The woodsy scent of his aftershave was intoxicating as he dropped a brief, warm kiss on her cheek. She stood transfixed feeling as if it were her first time in a boardroom.

All because of a handsome face, she thought, disgusted with herself and so very glad that her sister Genevieve wasn't here to see this.

In Antonio's eyes she saw a hint that he knew how he'd rattled her. She forced herself to kiss his cheek and totally ignored the fact that the five o'clock shadow on his jaw made her lips tingle.

She stepped back and retrieved her hand. "I only have twenty minutes to talk to you, Signore Moretti."

"Then I had better talk fast," he said with a grin.

She fought to keep her face stoic. She could see that he was charming. He wasn't trying hard; he just seemed unflappable.

She was too. She had spent her entire life being the reliable sister. The one that her father and grandfather could count on. She wasn't going to be a disappointment to them the way her great-aunt Anna had been when she'd lost Lorenzo's attention and the family name.

"I don't really see the point to this meeting. As you know, Moretti Motors has resigned all rights to the Vallerio name when you let that contract lapse. At this time we aren't inclined to license it to you again."

"You have not even heard what we are offering."

"I don't need to. You have nothing we want," Nathalie said. But she was interested in hearing what they were offering. Even her father thought that the Morettis must realize that they couldn't come to the bargaining table without offering substantial compensation. Her father wanted a half share in Moretti Motors. To be honest, Nathalie was confident they'd never go for that and she thought this entire exercise was one big time waster.

But she was here because her father had asked her to try to get this deal on the table. That was the problem with family feuds, she thought. There were never really any winners. No matter what deal she and Antonio negotiated.

"Are you sure about that? Everyone wants something they can't have," Antonio said.

"Well, if they can't have it, then they are just asking for frustration," Nathalie said.

"*Touché*. But I'm offering you whatever you want."

"Anything, Signore Moretti?"

"*Sì*, Nathalie. But you are going to have to do something before we can go any further with these negotiations."

Nathalie liked the way he said her name. The Americans she was used to dealing with didn't know the right emphasis to place on it the way Antonio did. "What is that?"

"You must stop calling me Signore Moretti. I am Antonio to my business associates and Tony to my intimates."

"Very well, Antonio."

He laughed and she found herself smiling. She liked this man and she hadn't expected to. From reputation she knew he usually won most of his corporate encounters, but then so did she and she'd expected him to be like other men.

She was pleasantly surprised to see that he wasn't. She had to remember that he was being charming for only one reason. He wanted something from her and he wasn't planning on taking no for an answer.

Antonio seldom met a woman he couldn't easily charm, but then he seldom met a woman who blinded him with only her smile. It didn't matter that there was something about Nathalie that said she saw through him. He tried to keep his eyes on business, but all he could think of was how soft her skin had felt when he'd shaken her hand and kissed her cheek.

He wanted to kiss her lips, to feel that full lush mouth under his. Every time she spoke he felt a little jab as she no doubt intended him to. He'd known from the moment he set up this meeting that negotiations between the Vallerio family and the Moretti family weren't going to be easy.

All of the research he'd done on Nathalie had helped him form the opinion that this was a woman who wasn't going to be easily swayed by charm.

Seduction, as Dom had suggested, wouldn't work either. She was too smart and she watched him carefully, adjusting her plan of action to fit his.

"Have a seat, Nathalie. And we will see if I can't find something the Vallerio family will take in exchange for letting us use the name that your grandfather made famous."

Nathalie brushed past him, her scent clean and refreshing, and sat down at the head of the table. He bit the inside of his cheek to keep from smiling. It was obvious to him that she was used to being in charge.

He was the type of man who didn't like to let anyone take the lead. But he knew sitting at the head of the table didn't give one power. Power came from the person who wielded it.

Nathalie too knew that, he suspected. She'd learned it from her grandfather. Pierre-Henri Vallerio was a proud French F1 driver who loved racing, designing cars and, at the end of his life, anything that would upset Lorenzo Moretti—the man who had once been his best friend and his teammate on the F1 circuit for Team Moretti.

"Antonio, we do want something from Moretti Motors," she said.

"Of course you do," he said. "I'm here to make sure we both get what we want."

"*Bien.* Vallerio Incorporated wants half share in all of the profits from Moretti Motors and seventy percent of the profit from the Vallerio production model. We also want the right to change the styling of the Vallerio trademark."

Antonio shook his head. "I said we'd negotiate, not give away everything my brothers and I have worked to rebuild. What we are offering is a share in the profits from the Vallerio model and a seat on the board for the head of Vallerio Incorporated."

"Êtes-vous fou?"

"No, I'm not crazy. We think this offer is very generous."

She shook her head. "Of course you do. You are used to holding all the cards, but in this case, you must realize that you do not. Without the Vallerio name, you cannot release your new production car."

"Of course we can, Nathalie. We'd just have to rename it, which we are prepared to do if need be," Antonio said. He wasn't lying. It was a car that everyone talked about.

And they wanted to recapture the magic that *Nono* had first discovered with Moretti Motors.

"Then I suggest you start redesigning your car. As you know you can't use the name or any likeness to the original Vallerio Roadster."

She pushed to her feet and reached for her designer leather briefcase and he knew that this woman wasn't going to be an easy opponent. And damn if that didn't excite the hell out of him.

"Nathalie, we are just starting our talks. There is no need to get up from the table yet."

She shook her head, that beautiful red hair swinging gently around the shoulders of her conservative black Chanel suit that accented her curves. "Are you willing to meet our terms?"

"No, I am not. We can talk about a small share of profits for your company, but it won't be fifty percent."

"I'm afraid that our terms aren't really negotiable," Nathalie said.

"Then why are you here? You know that we won't agree to give you that kind of money."

"You asked for this meeting, Antonio. No one on the board at Vallerio Incorporated cares much for Moretti Motors. They would rather have Grandfather's name drop into obscurity than license its use to your family."

Antonio leaned back in the leather chair and thought about Nathalie. He couldn't keep just turning on the charm and hoping that would crack her composure.

She was smart and willing to stand her ground, so that meant he was going to have to reevaluate how he dealt with her.

"Why are you staring at me like that?" she asked. She rubbed her fingers over her lips and then tucked a strand of hair behind her ear.

"Am I staring?"

She tipped her head to the side. "You know you are."

"Indeed I am. I am looking for a chink in your

armor. Trying to figure out what makes you tick," he said, knowing that honesty was a very powerful tool in the boardroom because so many of his opponents often felt the virtue overrated.

She nibbled on her lower lip. "I don't have any chinks."

He threw his head back and laughed at her bravado. Damn, but he liked this woman. If she wasn't a Vallerio he'd even ask her out, but he knew that his family and hers had bad karma between them. And despite what he'd said to Dom earlier, he didn't want to take the chance that *Nono*'s bad woman mojo might touch him.

"I like the way you laugh," she said.

"Really? Why is that?"

"It makes you seem human."

He wanted to laugh again. "I am human, Nathalie. Do not ever doubt that."

"Well, your reputation would say otherwise."

"What does my reputation say about me?"

She leaned forward, bracing her arms on the table. The movement caused her blouse to hang away from her skin and he saw the briefest hint of the curve of her breast. He wondered if he should follow Dom's advice and seduce Nathalie—not to win the negotiation but because he wanted her.

"Well, the gossip about is that you are cold-blooded when it comes to business."

"I've heard the same thing about you," he said. And he had. She was known as the Ice Queen, and men that had dealt with Vallerio Incorporated spoke of her in unkind terms, often using words like *bitch*.

"That simply isn't true," she said.

"Then what is the truth about you?" he asked.

"I just believe that all is fair in love and war," she said.

"Me too."

"Well, then we are evenly matched and I'd say let the war begin."

Two

Nathalie knew exactly how she'd come to be sitting at Cracco Peck on Via Victor Hugo in the City Centre of Milan later that evening. She'd never met a man who was uniquely suited to her. But Antonio was.

He was smart, savvy and sexy as hell and she knew that no matter what the outcome, she was going to enjoy her negotiations with him. She liked being with him because unlike the previous lawyers she had dealt with, he didn't seem to resent that she was a strong woman.

He was several yards away talking to the chef-owner, Carlo Cracco, which allowed her to study him unabashedly. He had an easy way about him, and she realized the charm that she'd first noticed in the Moretti conference room was a part of him, not something he turned on strictly for women.

"Nathalie?"

She smiled as she stood up to greet an old family friend, Fredrico Marchessi.

"*Buona sera,* Fredrico," she said, kissing him warmly on the cheek. He had been at the university with her father. "Is Maria with you?"

"I'm afraid not. This is a business trip for me."

"For me as well," she said.

"With the Moretti family?"

"*Oui,* Fredrico."

"Your father is worried about this," Fredrico said.

Nathalie got annoyed at the way Fredrico talked to her as if she were still twelve. She'd been successfully handling the Vallerio family business for a number of years now.

"Papa knows he can trust me to do what is right by our family."

"*Bien,* Nathalie. We must have dinner when you are back in Paris."

"*Bien sur.* I will call your office."

Fredrico left and she felt a hand on her back as she started to sit back down. Antonio was back at their table.

"Nathalie, allow me to introduce you to Carlo Cracco."

They exchanged pleasantries and then the chef left and she was alone with Antonio at the intimate table for two.

"I am sorry for leaving you alone."

"It's okay," she said. "I'm not your date."

"And if you were?"

"Well, then I'd expect you to not leave me alone. A woman deserves to be the center of her man's attention."

"What does a man deserve?"

"The same thing."

"Are you a romantic?" he asked.

She shook her head. "No. I just don't believe in wasting my personal time with someone who's not worth it."

He gave her that crooked grin, revealing his straight white teeth. "Another point we agree on."

She shrugged one shoulder, trying not to acknowledge that Antonio was the kind of man she didn't believe existed. Someone who could be her equal in the boardroom and out of it. "What did your chef friend recommend for dinner?"

"I've never been disappointed with anything I've ordered here. My favorite dish is salt-crusted sole and dark chocolate crochettes with caviar."

She pretended to study the menu. This meeting was supposed to be about the Vallerio family. She had to concentrate and keep reminding herself that her family had been waiting for this moment for a long time. No matter how much she enjoyed the novelty of Antonio Moretti.

He was just that. A novelty. This was nothing more than a chance for her grandfather to even the score with Lorenzo Moretti, even though the latter was long gone from this world. Her grandfather wouldn't have a moment's peace until he knew that he'd been able to retrieve the honor that Lorenzo had swindled him out of.

"You look very serious, *mia cara*. Would it be so bad to let me recommend a dish for you?" He named two selections.

She looked up at him. "I see you are the type of man who will exploit any sign of weakness in your opponent."

"I thought we were beyond pointless shows of power."

Was that what he thought this was? She was always aware that she was a woman in a man's world and that she couldn't for a minute appear weak. She never cried, she didn't chat or laugh with the other women in the office and she certainly didn't let a man order for her at a business dinner. That was too feminine, too girly, and she knew a man's man like Antonio Moretti would see it as a sign of weakness.

"Thanks for the recommendations. I'll consider them."

He laughed. "You do that."

The wine steward arrived and Nathalie again felt the pressure of their roles. The steward automatically talked to Antonio about the wine selection, and even though he selected the exact vintage she would have chosen, she spoke up and picked something different.

Meals and drinks ordered, she sat back at the table and took control of this evening. "Tell me more about the Moretti Motors plans for the Vallerio model."

"I can only share so much information with you before we hammer out an arrangement. As I am sure you can understand, it's privileged."

"Of course. Tell me why we should even consider doing business with the Moretti family again. The last time we did my beloved great-aunt Anna was destroyed by her dealings with your grandfather and my own grandfather was swindled out of his share of the profits."

The feud between their families had at its heart the emotions of a young bride. Decades ago her *tante* Anna had married her brother's best friend—Lorenzo Moretti—and then found herself ignored and very unhappy. Lorenzo was a womanizer and Anna spent three miserable years married to him before she left him, something that Lorenzo didn't even realize for another six months. It was that treatment of Anna that had started the feud. When Anna divorced Lorenzo, something that left her ostracized from her devoutly Catholic community in Paris, Lorenzo had terminated production of the Vallerio Roadster, saying that he wouldn't share profits with a family that had betrayed him.

He felt Anna should have sucked up her hurt feelings and stayed with him.

"You make us sound like the Machiavellis. I assure you we aren't."

"Assurances are okay, Antonio, but I'd rather have some facts that I can take back to my board of directors."

"How about the fact that Vallerio Incorporated hasn't had a new innovation in the car world in over twenty years?"

"We know what our history is," she said. "We aren't in the automobile world anymore."

"Which is why you are here with me. The Vallerio-Moretti collaboration went all wrong last time. Our generation will be the ones to put both of our family names back into the limelight and give them the place in history they deserve."

* * *

Milan was vibrant and alive on this cool spring night and Antonio took a deep breath as he led Nathalie through the center of town to the Piazza del Duomo.

He knew the key to getting the Vallerio team to sign the deal was to break down the monster that his *nono* had become to them. And this square was the very place to do that.

"Why did you bring me here?" Nathalie asked. She seemed a little tired and a little leery.

He hoped to use that to his advantage. "I wanted you to understand why history is so important to us at Moretti Motors.

"I know that the Vallerio family harbors some bad feelings toward the Moretti family, but I believe that that stems simply from misunderstanding the man that my grandfather was."

Nathalie tipped her head to the side. Her red-gold hair swung against her shoulder and distracted him, made him want to touch the cool silky waves.

"Your grandfather may have had another side, but I doubt he showed it to anyone outside of the Moretti clan."

"Then let me tell you about him now."

Nathalie sighed. "Do you really believe this will make a difference?"

Antonio looked at her standing there in the moonlight and knew that even if it didn't he wanted to tell her about his family. He wanted to change the image she had in her head of the Morettis as the big bad guys. "When I was a boy I'd come to Milan to visit my *nono,* he'd bring me here to church every morning. He never missed a day."

"My *grandpere* was the same way. He said it was because God had blessed him on the racetrack," Nathalie said.

Antonio smiled to himself. *Nono* had told him how Pierre-Henri had been a devout man. It was one of the few positive things that *Nono* had ever mentioned about Pierre-Henri. Lorenzo Moretti had known from an early age that the Lord watched over him each time he got in his race car and attempted things no other man had ever done.

"See? We already have something in common."

She arched one eyebrow at him. "Really? That's the connection you are going to make?"

"In this battle, with the stakes being what they are, I'll start as small as I have to."

"Why do you want this so bad? As you said, Moretti Motors can rename the car."

"Because Moretti Motors' Vallerio Roadster is revered by car collectors all over the world. The demand for this model, the styling and racing lines that Lorenzo designed along with Pierre-Henri's engine design are legendary."

"So you do need us?" she asked.

"Maybe."

Antonio took Nathalie's hand and drew her closer to the cathedral. "Did you know that Duomo here has never really been completed?"

She shook her head. "I don't know that much about this church."

"I won't tell you the history, only that she is constantly being updated and added to. The church itself is never going to be finished because there is always some way to improve on its beauty, to improve on its function.

"It is the same for Moretti Motors. We are not content to sit around and think that we have accomplished one thing and that is enough. We must constantly change, constantly drive forward into the future. What we are offering you, Nathalie, and the entire Vallerio family and its investors is a chance to be a part of our drive to the future."

Nathalie drew her hand free of his. "You are a smooth talker, you know that, right?"

"*Sì*," he said with a smile. "I think you like that about me."

"I like a lot about you, Antonio. But that doesn't

mean that I think doing business with your company would be in our best interests."

"Why not?" he asked.

She walked around the entrance to the cathedral. The statues that guarded it looked down upon them. This cathedral was one of the most famous in the world, the second largest to St. Peter's Basilica in Rome itself. Every Catholic in Milan was proud that this was their house of worship, and Antonio offered a quick prayer that God would make this moment a turning point for him and Moretti Motors.

"*Grandpere* used to say that Lorenzo was a smooth-tongued devil who had a way of seducing even the staunchest rival," she said. "And I can see now what he meant. I think you inherited Lorenzo's charm."

"You should meet my father."

"I guess all of the Moretti men have that gift. Do you know what we Vallerios have?"

"A gift for speed and a quest for knowledge," he said. The legacy of Pierre-Henri wasn't one that he took lightly. That was one of the main reasons why he, Marco and Dominic had decided to go this route. They could have taken an easier path with relaunching their production car, but the only car they wanted to relaunch was the Vallerio.

"We also have a way of seeing through the smoke and mirrors to the truth behind them," she said.

"Keep looking, Nathalie. There is nothing but truth and sincerity here. At Moretti Motors we want both of our companies to grow and prosper. We want both of our names to be remembered by history."

"You paint a pretty picture, Antonio, almost as pretty as this Gothic cathedral you've brought me to see, but I know that inside the walls of this place and behind the beauty of your offer lie more secrets."

"In the church perhaps, but I have laid all my cards on the boardroom table."

"Somehow I doubt that. It would leave you with nothing new to negotiate with."

He laughed at that. "Well, maybe I've kept one or two back."

"I have too. I'm not going to change my position tonight. To be honest I doubt we will ever be able to reach an agreement. There is too much bad blood between our families."

"But not between us. That was two stubborn old men who liked to argue. We are two young, vibrant people who know that there is more to life than fighting," Antonio said.

"Do we?"

"Yes, Nathalie, we do," he said, and drew her into his arms. "The night is young and so are we. Let's make the most of it."

* * *

At the end of the evening Antonio walked her back to her hotel. She was tired but pleasantly so. She had enjoyed the evening with him and she understood now what real charm was.

Her *grandpere* had been a brusque man by the time she'd gotten to know him, and a part of her was saddened by that. And she knew that the Moretti family—especially Lorenzo Moretti—was responsible for his bitterness.

But right now, as Antonio walked her to her room, that didn't seem to matter.

She knew starting an affair with Antonio Moretti was about the dumbest thing she could do. But she was so tempted.

They stood right outside her suite and though she had the feeling it would be unwise, she wanted to invite him in for a nightcap.

Antonio broke into her thoughts. "You are looking at me like I have something you want."

"You do."

"Name it and it is yours."

She tipped her head to the side. "Did you mean it when you said that all's fair in love and war?"

"Yes, I did."

"You aren't going to renege on that?"

"No, I'm not. Are you?"

"No. But I've found that men get mad when they don't win, regardless of what they've said before everything got going."

"I think you are trying to ask me if I'm going to act like a baby if I don't get my way. You should know that I am a man…not a boy."

She smiled at the way he said it. She knew Antonio was trying to seduce her. He wanted her to get to know the man behind the corporation and it was in her interest to do the same. Let him get to know the woman she was. Without that she'd never get the advantage over him.

"So, *bella mia,* are you going to tell me what you want?"

"Maybe."

"Maybe?"

"I think being mysterious has some benefits," she said.

"Indeed it does in a woman as beautiful as you."

She suspected that comment was at least seventy-five percent bullshit, but… "It's hard to resist such charm."

He laughed again, his deep, melodious tones wrapping around her in a dangerous way. She knew she needed to get rid of Antonio. She wasn't going to invite him in tonight, not after an evening of a full moon shining down over the city as she listened to him weave his tales of the past in that deeply erotic voice of his. Tonight she wasn't up to sparring with him.

Her plan was to let him think *he* seduced *her* and she wasn't sure yet if she could sleep with this man and keep her emotions at bay.

To be honest she'd never been able to do that.

"Good night, Antonio."

"I will see you first thing in the morning for a tour of the Moretti Motors facility."

"I'm not sure—"

"You already agreed to it," he said. "It will do you good to meet the people who have worked on the design of the Vallerio model. I think you should see the pride that our workers take in being part of that legendary car."

"I think you should stop referring to the car as the Vallerio."

"Of course. It's just that I feel that once you see this car you will change your mind."

His passion for the car and for the company was obvious and it made her realize she'd made the right choice in not inviting him into her room. She had to understand that with Antonio the company was always going to come first.

And Nathalie had a personal vow about men who were workaholics. She'd never get mixed up with one. Her father, uncles and grandfather all had been workaholics—and had been absent in the lives of their children and wives, something that Nathalie didn't want for her own life.

Not that she was thinking of having kids with Antonio. It was just that getting involved with a man when you knew you were destined to be second in his life was not a smart thing to do.

And she was a smart woman.

She met Antonio's gaze and nodded. "I like your confidence. Tomorrow we will see if you are simply bragging or if you have the goods."

He arched one eyebrow at her. "*Cara mia,* do I look like a man who doesn't have the goods?"

She shook her head. "I refuse to answer that on the grounds that no matter what answer I give you, you will take it as a positive."

Antonio shrugged his big shoulders. "I'm used to making everything into a positive. That is why Moretti Motors is where it is today."

"I'd heard that about you. That you never take no for an answer. Much like Lorenzo Moretti when he ran right over Anna Vallerio."

"That is very true about my not taking no for an answer. But I promise you, Nathalie, I'm not going to run over you or your family. This generation of Moretti Motors is committed to doing business differently."

He walked away on that note and she watched him leave. She wanted to believe his words, but at the end of the day Antonio was still a Moretti. And he was going to put those interests before her or her family.

Three

Antonio's mobile phone rang as soon as he pulled out of the parking lot of Nathalie's hotel. He glanced at the caller ID. Damn. His brother was very well connected in Milan—hell, they all were—but if Dom was seriously following his moves that closely, then there was more at stake than just the Vallerio car model.

"*Buona sera,* Dom."

"How'd the meeting with Ms. Vallerio go?"

Dom wasn't one of those guys who wasted time on small talk. There had been a leak in their office over the last year and though they had gotten closer to the snitch, they still hadn't found him. Something that Antonio knew annoyed Dom to no end.

"Fine."

"I'd say better than fine. Genaro said that you were upstairs with her for more than thirty minutes."

"Gee, Dom, I hope that you don't think I seduced her in thirty minutes."

"Well…it is a little quick, but I figured you might have your mind on other things."

"No wonder your relationships don't last longer than a tank of gas. Women want to be seduced by a man. They want a man who will linger and act interested in them."

"Which is neither here nor there. What did she say?" Dom asked.

Antonio activated the hands-free option that was built into his GPS.

"Can you hear me?"

"Yes," Dom said. "What happened?"

"We talked. The Vallerio family isn't going to be easy. Are you sure we need his name?"

"I'm going to pretend I didn't hear that," Dom said.

"I just wanted to make sure. The negotiations are going to be long and hard on this one, and right now we don't need that."

That was an understatement. Not only was the

production date breathing down their necks, but they still hadn't identified the leak in their office.

As if he read his mind, Dom said, "I am close to figuring out the leak. I have set some things in motion now that will take care of it."

"What things?" Antonio asked.

"More proprietary information given only to two people. I've almost narrowed it down. If I'm right about who it is, it's going to be someone close to us."

"Whom do you suspect?" Antonio asked, not even thinking about the Vallerio business for a minute. Corporate espionage was a big deal and the leaks they had lately were enough to seriously cripple Moretti Motors.

"I'd rather not say at this moment. I'll take care of the leak. You just do what you need to with Vallerio. So, if you didn't seduce the girl, what's your plan?"

Antonio had turned onto the street where he lived. He had a nice place with assigned parking on the street. There were times when he wished he had the space his parents did in their palatial house outside of the city limits, but he liked city living.

He switched his phone back to the handset and got out of the car. His street was quiet this late at night.

"My plan is the same as it always is. Find her weakness and then use it to our advantage," Antonio said. Though for the first time he was torn. He really did believe that all was fair in love and war, but this time he didn't know that he wanted to exploit the weaknesses he found in Nathalie. He would, he knew, but this time he might regret it.

"Her weakness or Vallerio's?" Dom asked.

"Aren't they the same?" Antonio asked.

"In most cases I'd say yes, but if you are going to seduce the girl, then I imagine your thinking could get muddled."

"I have to remember that. There is no gray area here."

"Don't let Nathalie get her hooks in you. I don't think *Nono's* legacy is going to withstand two of us falling in love."

"So you don't believe that Marco and Virginia have broken the curse?" Antonio asked. He had read the words of Cassia Festa's curse in the journal that Virginia had. He thought about the curse he'd read.

My love for you was all-encompassing and never ending and with its death I call upon the universe to bring about the death of your heart and the hearts of succeeding generations.

As long as a Moretti roams this earth, he shall have happiness in either business or love but never both. Do not disdain the power of my small body. Moretti, you may be strong, but that will no longer help you. I am strong in my will and I demand retribution for the pain you have caused me.

Virginia might have broken the curse for Marco by combining Festa and Moretti blood, but Antonio wasn't too sure.

Dom replied, "Maybe as far as Marco is concerned they have, but I have the feeling you and I aren't out of the woods yet."

"You better be careful, old man. I would never be so weak as to fall for any woman."

"That's what Marco thought."

"Our baby brother was distracted by the races. I am not about to be."

"Remember that, Tony. We are on the cusp of taking Moretti Motors to heights that it has never seen before," Dom said.

Antonio knew that better than anyone. He and his brothers had been born to a legacy of both pride and powerful determination but also to the curses that Lorenzo Moretti had left behind. This mess with the Vallerio family was only one of them. If Dom was right and Marco managed to appease the curse put on them by Cassia Festa, Lorenzo's spurned lover, then thank the stars. The fact that no generation of

Moretti men had ever been lucky in business and in love wasn't going to be easily forgotten by either himself or Dom.

"Do I have your permission to act without checking in?" Antonio asked.

"Why?"

"I might need to act quickly to get Nathalie to agree."

"Nathalie?"

"Ms. Vallerio."

"Yes, you can act without checking in with the board. I will back you. But make sure that you get the results we need, Tony."

"Have I failed you yet?"

"No. No, you haven't."

He rang off with his brother and entered his house. The town house was opulently decorated and quiet at this time of night. He had never noticed the silence of the place before, but tonight with Dom's words echoing in his head and after the evening he'd spent with Nathalie, he wondered if he, like *Nono,* was doomed to spend his life alone.

Nathalie had a restless night's sleep and woke early. She stood on the balcony of her hotel suite and looked out over the city of Milan. In the distance she saw Duomo and heard the bells of the cathedral still calling the faithful to worship. She touched the small gold cross at her neck and thought of her father.

He wanted her to succeed because it had been his aunt who had been so badly used by Lorenzo, and his father who had been duped by his onetime friend.

She took a sip of her cappuccino and leaned back in the cushioned wrought-iron chair. Her family wasn't used to failing. After their disastrous business deal with Lorenzo Moretti, the Vallerios had made it their mission to never walk away from any deal the loser.

And Nathalie followed a proud tradition of being the one to make sure that her family won.

There was a knock on her hotel door and she glanced at her watch to check the time. It was too early to be anyone from Moretti's office coming to check on her.

She walked across the room with a feeling of dread. The timing was exactly right for someone to arrive if they'd taken the early flight from Paris.

She checked the peephole and groaned out loud.

"Papa, what are you doing here?" she asked as she opened the door.

Emile Vallerio crossed the threshold and kissed her on both cheeks. "We wanted to make sure that everything was okay here in Milan."

"We?"

Like magic, her sister appeared in the doorway. "I decided to come with Papa to see if I could help out in any way," Genevieve said.

Nathalie's older sister was renowned for her beauty and charm. Nathalie had never really minded being the smart sister, but if her father had brought Genevieve he must think... "Why?"

"Let's discuss this over coffee. I see you aren't ready for your meeting."

"Papa, I've been handling these things for a long time. I don't need you and Genevieve here. I can handle it. Go back to Paris."

"We will. After we are sure you know what you are doing," Emile said.

"I love you both very much, but I don't need you to tell me how to do my job."

"I know," Genevieve said. "But the Morettis can be tricky."

"I'm not untried. I can handle Antonio," she said, wondering if the words were true. Could she handle him? Last night had tested her and she suspected each day they spent together in the boardroom was going to make resisting him more difficult.

"Antonio?" Genevieve questioned.

"How is he in person? I've heard that he's a shark," Emile said.

"He's a lot like me. I think we'll get some of the

things we want, but we're not going to be able to rake them over the coals as you might have wanted."

"At the end of the day, I just want a fair deal for our family. Lorenzo manipulated my aunt out of her share of the Moretti fortune. We don't want that for this generation. She was promised a share of Moretti Motors and in order to get Lorenzo to sign the annulment so she could marry again he made her give up her rights to those shares."

"I agree, Papa. I've told Antonio that we aren't going to take just any deal. There's nothing in this for us unless they sweeten their offer."

She glanced down at her watch. "I have to start getting ready."

"Go ahead," her father said. "We will wait here for you."

She rolled her eyes. She knew how important this was to her family. Her great-aunt had been in a bitter marriage and had died young. They had almost no contact with her son and his family. The split of the Vallerio and Moretti families was complete.

"What are you going to wear today?" her sister asked.

"I don't need fashion advice, Genie."

"I know. But this man is used to very sophisticated women."

Her sister had a point. She was used to winning

in the boardroom based on her smarts and her determination. But with Antonio, maybe she could use
clothing and feminine wiles to distract him.

She sighed. "What do you think I should wear?"

Genevieve laughed. "I took the liberty of bringing
a dress with me that I think will look super on you."

"Do you really think so?" Nathalie asked. In this
case she deferred to the pretty sister.

"Nat, you goof, of course it will. You probably
already have him dazzled. This is just going to take
away his ability to look anywhere but at your cleavage."

She shook her head. "I don't like to use my body
as a tool."

"Why not? Nature made us this way, Nat. We're
not stronger than men but we are smarter." Genevieve winked. "And sexier."

"You haven't met Antonio."

"Really?"

"Yes," she said. "He's very sexy."

"Good. Then he'll use his looks to his benefit. You
won't be taking advantage of him by bringing sex
into the boardroom."

Her sister had a point. And Antonio had agreed that
all was fair in love and war. And this most definitely
was war, she thought. Last night he'd pushed the
boundaries of the attraction between them. Normally
Nathalie wouldn't try to be some sort of femme fatale,

but in this instance and with Genevieve's help she had the feeling she couldn't lose.

The meeting went long into the afternoon. Everyone else looked tired and frustrated, but Nathalie looked more beautiful than when she'd first come to the Moretti Motors building this morning.

Her father and sister were also at the table, and Dom had joined them when he'd realized there were more Vallerios in here other than just Nathalie.

"Let's take a break," Antonio suggested. "We need to all stretch and get some air. I've asked my staff to set up some drinks in the garden."

"I don't think fresh air is going to resolve the issues on the table," Emile said.

Nathalie's father had the same sharp intelligence as his daughter but none of her charm. He was still angry with Lorenzo and because of that he was a liability at the negotiating table. He sensed Nathalie knew it, but how did one tell a family member to get lost? He knew it couldn't be done. When family and business were mixed, there was no way to win.

"I realize that, Emile. I thought a break will give us all a chance to regroup and then get back to work."

"Sounds good," Dom said. "My assistant, Angelina, will lead you to the garden."

"Where will you be?"

"In my office," Dom said. "Antonio and I need a moment and then we'll be right down."

Angelina led the Vallerio family out of the boardroom and he turned to Dom. "What did you need to discuss?"

"That Emile is an ass. I don't see the point to all of this. His only agenda seems to be to taunt us with the fact that we can't use his father's name."

"I know. Give me a few minutes to think this over."

"I already have. Screw them. We are going to use Marco's name instead. He's made a name for himself on Grand Prix. One that even Pierre-Henri didn't have."

"But he doesn't have the cachet that Pierre-Henri does, thanks to that roadster he helped design and gave his name to. No matter that Pierre-Henri drove for our team—Team Moretti. The Vallerios think they are owed more than the compensation they were given. And because of the way *Nono* treated Anna Vallerio, I guess Emile is right to feel that way."

Dom stood up and walked over to the floor-to-ceiling windows and looked down into the courtyard garden where the Vallerio family was assembled. "I'm not going to play Emile's game. Whatever *Nono* did to his aunt, we're not responsible for it. This is business, not revenge."

"I'm not ready to throw in the towel yet. I need

some time alone with Nathalie. We both are sea-
soned at negotiating so I'm sure we can get to something workable."

"Not if her father is in the room. And why is the
sister here? She didn't add a single thing."

"I have no idea. Why don't you offer to take them
on a tour of the factory and show them the mock-up
of the new Vallerio? That will give me a chance to
talk to Nathalie privately."

"I think I'll have Angelina take care of that."

"You can't. Emile will be offended if it's not you
or I doing the tour. I think it's important that we give
him his due here. What *Nono* did to the Vallerios…well, from their perspective wasn't right."

"We didn't exactly prosper from his actions either.
But I understand what you're saying. I'll do my part.
It's just Marco's luck that he's not here."

"He will be next week and then we can send him
to deal with Emile and Genevieve."

"But not Nathalie?"

"No. I'm the one who can handle her."

"Are you sure? You seemed distracted a few times."

He had been distracted. Yesterday he'd been
struck by Nathalie's brains and wit more than her
looks. But today she'd pulled out all the stops and
he couldn't help but remember how she'd felt in his
arms the night before.

"It was nothing. I can handle Nathalie," Antonio said. "Any word on the leak?"

"No. Nothing. But the information I am using as bait is highly sensitive and I don't think we'll hear about it for a few days."

"Should we bring in an outside company?"

"I thought of that. I hired Stark Services to help."

"Good. I like Ian and he's not afraid to go for blood. He sees corporate spying as a real international crime."

"I agree. He's going to get stuff we can use in court."

"Good. Does he know about the bait?"

"Yes, it was his suggestion. He's on his way here from London. We should see him in the offices in the next day or so."

Ian Stark had been a college friend of Dom's and he'd gone into his family's business of protecting the rich and famous. Not as a bodyguard but as an intellectual properties security officer. He protected the secrets of the famous and he did a damn fine job of it.

"I'm glad Ian's working for us."

Dom shrugged. "I was hoping to handle it ourselves, but I'm not taking any chances on this."

Antonio knew that. He felt the same way. There was something about going from moving in wealthy circles to being beholden on their wealthier relatives that had cemented in all his brothers the belief that success was the most important thing in life. Money might not be able to buy happiness, but it did buy security and that was a very important commodity.

"We've come too far to fail now," Antonio said.

Dom looked him straight in the eye and smiled. "True enough."

"You seem relieved to hear me say that."

"Sometimes I feel like I forced my dreams on both you and Marco."

Antonio shook his head. As teenaged boys, Marco, Dominic and he had made a vow to never fall in love. They had promised and sealed it with blood that they would be the generation to be lucky in business. "We took that blood oath together, remember? We all want this."

"Yeah, until a pretty face comes along."

"I think that little Enzo won Marco over as much as Virginia did," Antonio said.

Dom shrugged. "If he broke that curse on our family I'll be happy, but I'm not convinced."

"Me either. I know that Virginia thinks the mingling of their blood broke it, but I remember that she said that they couldn't fall in love. That seems like a mighty big oops on their behalf," Antonio said. "Not that I've ever put much stock in the curse."

"That's because you've never been in love."

"Nor tempted to be," Antonio said. "Women are meant to be enjoyed and savored but never permanently."

Dom's mobile rang and he stepped into the hall to answer it. Antonio straightened his papers on the boardroom table and felt someone watching him. He glanced up to see Nathalie standing there.

"So women are like chocolates?" she asked.

"I never said that. Just that men and women seldom want things for the long haul."

"What about your parents?"

"They are the exception to the rule. And I'm not sure that they would have survived as a couple if my papa was interested in business."

"I'm not following," she said.

"I'm the kind of man who is all or nothing, so a woman could never compete with my business interests."

She nodded. "That's good to know."

Four

Nathalie had come back upstairs to see if she could have a minute of Antonio's time. His brother and her father were both so stubborn and not at all suited to the kind of discussions that needed to happen if they were going to come to any sort of arrangement.

Hearing him say so baldly that love and forever with a woman was the last thing on his mind didn't really surprise her. From her experience, men couldn't have both a family and a successful career. Her father was interested in her and Genevieve only because they were involved in the family business.

Before they had graduated from college he'd only

been a distant figure, leaving their upbringing to their mother. Which Genevieve hadn't minded. But Nathalie always had. She'd craved her father's attention and from her earliest memory knew that the only way to get it was through Vallerio Inc.

"Dom is going to take your father and sister on a tour of the car factory so that we can have some time to talk about what we both want. I think together we can find a solution that will work for both of our families."

"I agree."

Nathalie did agree. She wanted this over with. She needed to finish up the negotiations in Milan and make her way back to Paris where her real life was. She didn't need to stay here under Antonio's influence any longer than necessary.

"Would you like to continue working in here?"

"Yes, I think it would be for the best."

"Okay, then, please have a seat."

Nathalie took the same seat she'd had before, expecting Antonio to sit across from her. Instead he took the seat right next to her.

"At the end of the day what will please Vallerio Inc.?"

"Besides our original offer?"

"Yes. You know I won't agree to those terms."

"I'm not sure. I know we want to make sure that the new Vallerio production car represents Pierre-

Henri's legacy. Profits are something we can haggle on, but *Grandpere*'s legendary status as a racer…I'd like to see that brought forward."

Antonio leaned closer, the scent of his aftershave surrounding her. Last night after he left she'd noticed that she still could smell and feel him around her. And she realized she was going to be feeling that until this business meeting was over.

"How do you want to handle that?" Antonio asked.

"He's already in the hall of fame, but I think I'd like to see the marketing campaign focus on why the car is named for my *grandpere*. I'd like him to be the focus and not Lorenzo."

Antonio made some notes on the yellow pad in front of him. His handwriting was scrawling and masculine.

"We can't leave Lorenzo out completely, but I'll see what we can do. What else do you want?"

"We will take the seat on the board that you offered."

"Of course."

"And we want profit sharing for our investors."

Antonio shook his head. "I'll have to talk to our board. Are you offering a reciprocal arrangement for our shareholders?"

"No. Why would I?"

"I don't know that we are going to go for it. What else do you want?"

"I'm still thinking seventy percent of the profits from the Vallerio Roadster."

"Well, you go back and see if you can get a reciprocal arrangement for us and I'll see about giving you fifty percent of the profits. Dom wanted to offer you guys thirty."

Nathalie jotted down a few notes. She thought she could talk the board and more importantly her father into accepting a fifty percent profit margin from the Vallerio production model. But the reciprocal deal…that was going to be harder. No one wanted another company to be a part of Vallerio Inc. On the other hand, they wouldn't turn down the money to be made from the roadster. R & D was expensive and they could always use more money for that. Though they didn't build cars, they developed engines and Vallerio Inc. was on the cusp of launching a new biofuel engine.

That was why they weren't too concerned about coming to an agreement with Moretti Motors for the Vallerio. The company stood to make huge profits from its groundbreaking engineering patent.

"I will have to go back and discuss it with my board. Why don't we reconvene in a couple of weeks?"

"You haven't heard what else we want," Antonio said.

"What else do you want?"

"If you can get your board to go for reciprocal profit sharing, then we'd like a seat on your board. Just so we can keep track of our investments."

"Antonio, let me be straight with you. The chances of us doing a reciprocal deal are slim."

"Then your shareholders should know they'll get no stake in the Vallerio Roadster."

She knew he wasn't going to give away the shop. And he knew at the end of the day that he wasn't going to give up until he had everything he wanted.

But then she remembered his comment from yesterday. *All's fair...* Pivoting her chair to face him, she leaned forward so that she was almost touching him. He glanced away from the table and down her body.

Inside she smiled. Genevieve's dress was right on the money and the perfect tool to distract Antonio. "I think we're both too tired to discuss this anymore today. How about if I send you an e-mail with the things we want?"

She was careful to keep her shoulders back so that her breasts were thrust forward. Inside she knew her business school mentor, Professor Stanley Muchen, would have told her that this behavior was deplorable.

But as Antonio leaned forward and took her hand in his she realized that she didn't care. She wanted to flirt with Antonio, and using her "wiles" to distract him was exactly what she needed to get what she wanted.

Nathalie suspected that Antonio wasn't paying as close attention to the meeting as he normally would have. She had to wonder if it was because of her new clothes. But that seemed a bit silly to her. Antonio was a sophisicated man who was used to attractive women.

But this wasn't like her normal boardroom maneuvering, and frankly, as Antonio leaned closer to her, she knew she was out of her league. The dress was just a costume she wore. It hadn't changed who she was on the inside. To be honest he knew she had no idea how to use her body to manipulate the deal.

"What are you thinking?" he asked.

"That I've started something I can't finish."

He stood up and leaned against the table in front of her. She arched her neck back to maintain eye contact.

"What do you mean, *cara?* This?" He gestured to the two of them.

"Yes, this. My sister said… Oh, man, am I really saying this out loud?"

"What did your sister say? That you should seduce me and get me to agree to all of your terms?"

She tipped her head to the side and realized that either he had thought of the idea of seducing her or someone on his team had suggested the same thing. "Perhaps."

"We are both adults, Nathalie," he said. "We are

attracted to each other. It doesn't have anything to do with our families or the companies they own."

She wished it were that easy. That she could simply turn off the corporate lawyer part of her brain and pretend that an affair with Antonio would have no repercussions beyond the emotional ones she felt when affairs ended.

"I'm trying to decide if you really believe that or if you are just trying another tactic to get me to agree to your terms," she said.

Antonio reached down and took her hand in his. "I always believe what I say. I might not tell you all the reasoning behind it, though."

"I am not sure—"

"Don't think about this, Nathalie. We both have agreed to go back to our board of directors and to discuss the new terms. There is nothing more to be said or done this day. Why not enjoy each other's company?"

"Why not?" she asked, shaking her head. "I imagine Romeo must have said the same thing to Juliet."

He laughed. "I don't intend for either of us to die and I'm pretty sure that Dom and Emile won't draw blood while touring the car factory."

"I'm not trying to be melodramatic. It's just we aren't two people whose paths have crossed without consequences. As much as I might want to have an affair with you—"

"You want to have an affair with me?" he asked, leaning forward.

Any other man would have been crowding her, but with Antonio he couldn't get close enough. She stood up and put her hands on his shoulders.

"You're a smart man. You can figure that out."

He reached up and touched the side of her face with one long finger and she shivered under that touch.

"I already have," he said, leaning up to rub his lips over hers.

She tunneled her fingers into his thick hair and held his head still. She wasn't about to let Antonio take control of any part of their relationship, and she had realized over the last few minutes that they were going to have a relationship. There was too much spark between them for her to ignore it. That wasn't true, she thought. She would have been able to ignore it if Antonio wasn't attracted to her.

But he was.

His tongue sliding over her lips made her entire body tingle. She tipped her head to the side and opened her mouth as he deepened the kiss. She had never reacted this quickly to a man before.

He tasted so good, so right. And for once everything about a man felt as though he was made for her.

He slid his hands down her back, stroking the length of her spine and then drawing her closer to him. As he sat there, she was nestled between his legs and felt the warmth of his body heat wrapping around her.

She pushed his suit coat off his shoulders and he shrugged out of it. She put her hands on his chest, wanting to feel his pulse beating under her fingers. She sucked his lower lip into her mouth and felt his hands flex against her hips. He lifted her up and set her on the table, then nudged her legs apart to make room between them for his hips.

The skirt of the dress she wore flowed over her thighs and onto the conference room table. She looked down at their bodies knowing that the time for talking was long gone.

"Antonio…"

"*Sì, la mia amore?*"

She realized she didn't know what to say. She wasn't going to call a halt to their lovemaking, so instead she took his face in both of her hands and brought their mouths together again. She kissed him with all the pent-up passion she'd carried for a lifetime. She refused to think of anything but this moment. Refused to occupy anything but his arms right now.

He groaned into her mouth and she felt his hands sweep up her sides to cup her breasts. She found his hips with her hands and drew him closer to her. She felt his erection nudging her center, but it only made her hungrier for him. She wanted—

A sound in the hallway made them pull apart. Antonio looked at her, something solid and steady in his eyes. Something she'd never really seen on a man's face before.

"I'm going to lock the door."

All she could do was nod because she knew she didn't want this moment to end.

Antonio locked the door and turned back to Nathalie. He knew the boardroom wasn't the place for this kind of encounter, but he couldn't wait to have Nathalie. Filled with the demands and pressures of their families as they were, he knew their coming together like this was a complication. Yet he couldn't walk away.

She looked so tempting with the sun streaming in from the tinted windows onto her red-gold hair. Her creamy pale skin was like a beacon, guiding him back to her. Unable to resist, he loosened his tie and hurried back to her side.

She was sitting just as he'd left her, her legs parted, those impossibly high peep-toe shoes on her tiny feet, the skirt of her dress draped over her thighs. Her breasts rose up and fell with her breaths.

"Lean back on your elbows for me, *cara*," he said.

She did as he asked. She was temptation incarnate, everything a man could want, and she wasn't doing anything but sitting there, just as she had all morning. She'd cast a spell over him just as powerful as the curse that Cassia Festa had put on Lorenzo all those years ago. But this spell was enchanting and he wanted nothing more than to indulge himself in her.

And he could. He wasn't going to deny himself the pleasure of Nathalie and her body.

Her green-gold eyes were shy as he tossed his tie on the credenza and unbuttoned his shirt, but once he touched her, took a strand of that red-gold hair of hers in his hand, all that melted away.

She stayed where he'd asked her to as he leaned down to take her mouth in his. She was the first woman he'd kissed who tasted like home to him.

She smelled of spring flowers and her skin was softer than anything he'd ever touched. He ran his hands down her arms, linking their fingers together as his mouth moved over hers.

He slid his hand down her side, finding the zipper hidden in the seam, and lowered it slowly. "I want you naked, *cara mia*."

"Me too, Antonio."

Blood rushed through his veins. Antonio knew the boardroom wasn't the sexiest place in the world, but with Nathalie that didn't matter. The fabric of her bodice gaped away from her chest and he wanted to see more.

"Arch your shoulders," he said.

"Like this?" Her shoulders moved and the loose bodice gaped further.

"What are you wearing under this?" he asked, tracing his finger along the seam where fabric met flesh.

"Why don't you find out?"

He growled deep in his throat. Leaning forward, he brushed soft kisses against her shoulder and collarbone, following the lines of her body down to where the loosened bodice was and then he took the soft fabric in his teeth and pulled it away from her skin. There was no strap from a bra there. Just the smooth skin of woman.

He pushed the fabric out of his way, letting it pool at her waist. She was exquisite, her breasts just the right size for her frame, her nipples a pretty pink accent to her creamy white skin. He hesitated to touch her, wanting to just look at her for a long moment.

"Take your shirt off," she said.

But he shook his head. "You do it."

She shifted on the table and reached between them, pushing his shirt off his shoulders. He took her wrists in his hands and drew them to his hips. He caressed the length of her arms and then slid his hands down her chest, caressing every bit of skin he touched.

"Come closer, Antonio."

"Like this?" He drew her into his arms, held her so her nipples brushed against the light dusting of hair on his chest.

"Yes."

He rotated his shoulders so that his chest rubbed against her breast. She squirmed delicately in his arms.

"I like that," she said.

Blood roared in his ears. He was so hard right now that he needed to be inside her body.

Impatient with the fabric of her dress, he shoved it up and out of his way. He caressed her creamy thighs. *Dio,* she was soft. She moaned as he neared her center and then sighed when he brushed his fingertips across the crotch of her panties.

The lace was warm and wet. He slipped one finger under the material and hesitated for a second, looking down into her eyes.

Her eyes were heavy lidded. She bit down on her lower lip and he felt the minute movements of her hips as she tried to move his touch where she needed it.

He was beyond teasing her or prolonging anything. He ripped her panties aside, plunged two fingers into her humid body. She squirmed against him.

He pulled her head down to his so he could taste

her mouth. Her mouth opened over his and he told himself to take it slow, but Nathalie was making him go naught to sixty in less than 3.5 seconds. She was pure fire. Like putting jet fuel in a car, she was sending him skyrocketing.

He nibbled on her and held her at his mercy. Her nails dug into his shoulders and she leaned up, brushing against his chest. Her nipples were hard points and he pulled away from her mouth, glancing down to see them pushing against his chest.

He caressed her back and spine, scraping his nail down the length of it. He followed the line of her back down the indentation above her backside.

She closed her eyes and held her breath as he fondled her, running his finger over her nipple. It was velvety compared to the satin smoothness of her breast. He brushed his finger back and forth until she bit her lower lip.

Her intelligence, wit and unwillingness to back down at the bargaining table had turned him on before, but seeing her today as a sexy, confident woman had been more than he could handle.

She moaned a sweet sound that he leaned up to capture in his mouth. She tipped her head to the side, allowing him access to her mouth. She held his shoulders and moved on him, rubbing her center over his erection.

He scraped his fingernail over her nipple and she shivered in his arms. He pushed her back a little bit so he could see her. Her breasts were bare, nipples distended and begging for his mouth. He lowered his head and suckled.

He held her still with a hand on the small of her back. He buried his other hand in her hair and arched her over his arm. Both of her breasts were thrust up at him. He had a lap full of woman and he knew that he wanted Nathalie more than he'd wanted any other woman in a long time.

Her eyes were closed, her hips moving subtly against him, and when he blew on her nipple he saw gooseflesh spread down her body.

He loved the way she reacted to his touch. He kept his attention on her breasts. Her nipples were so sensitive he was pretty sure he could bring her to an orgasm just from touching her there.

He suckled the inside of her left breast, needing to leave his mark on her so that later when she was away from him and surrounded by her family, she'd remember this.

He kept kissing and fondling her until her hands clenched in his hair and she rocked her hips harder against him. He lifted his hips, thrusting up against her. As he bit down carefully on her tender, aroused nipple, she screamed his name and he hurriedly covered her mouth with his, wanting to feel every bit of her passion.

He rocked her until the storm passed and she quieted in his arms. He held her close. Her bare breasts brushed against his chest. He was so hard he thought he'd die if he didn't get inside her.

Then he remembered he had no protection with him.

Maybe this time it was better to leave things as they were, he told himself. He'd just realized that keeping his head and his heart separate were going to be harder than he'd thought.

Damn, did he say heart? He wasn't the kind of man to fall for a woman. Even one as sexy as Nathalie Vallerio.

Five

Nathalie heard the door rattle a second before Antonio moved off her. She didn't regret what had just happened. How could she when every nerve ending in her body was still pulsing? But now the thought of getting caught horrified her.

"Mon dieu," she said.

"Shh, *cara mia*," he said, helping her off the table. Her dress started to fall down her body, but Antonio caught it and drew it back up her body. "We will finish this later."

She nodded. There was no way she'd deny herself an affair with this man now. She put herself to rights and turned to see he'd done the same. His shirt was buttoned and he had his tie back on.

"Antonio—"

"Shh. Say nothing now. We will talk later," he said, shrugging into his suit jacket.

She sat down in her chair and drew her notes to her, staring down at the table as if it held some kind of answer, but all she saw was what she should be focused on. Her family and the board of directors at Vallerio Inc. were expecting her to beat Antonio Moretti at this game. They'd expected her to get him to agree to her terms.

Instead she'd just been writhing in his arms. Even now she could fall into a simpering puddle at his feet because that had been the best orgasm of her life.

"Nathalie?"

"Hmm?" she asked, looking up to see Angelina standing there.

"Your family insists we accompany them on the tour of the factory."

"Very well. We had finished our discussion anyway," Nathalie said. She gathered her folders and put them into her leather briefcase.

"I can hold that for you at my desk, Ms. Vallerio," Angelina said.

The other woman was shorter than Nathalie with an hourglass figure that she showcased in her form-fitting sweater and pencil skirt. Angelina had big brown eyes and thick curly hair and a hesitant smile as she took the case from Nathalie.

"Thank you."

"My pleasure. They are waiting for you in the lobby of the factory, Antonio."

"*Grazie*, Angelina."

They left the boardroom together and Nathalie tried to force her mind to accept that nothing had changed between the two of them, but it had. The awkward silence between them underscored that for her.

"Antonio?"

"*Sì*, Nathalie?"

"I don't want this to interfere with our negotiations."

"It won't. I'm still going to be hard on you."

She had no doubt about that. Had she meant her words more for herself? Did she really need a reminder that she had made a mistake?

Had she?

Antonio hadn't been uninvolved and unless he was more of a playboy than his reputation indicated, she had to assume he felt something for her.

Did she use that to her advantage?

He paused to put on a pair of sunglasses and she wished she'd brought hers, for the midday sun in Milan was bright on this spring morning. He put his hand at the small of her back as they walked across the courtyard and she realized he'd fallen back into the mode that she needed to.

"I will send you an offer when I get back to Paris. It will expire in a week, Antonio. After that time we will no longer need to be in contact for the sake of our companies."

"What if I accept the offer you send?"

"I'm assuming you will," she said, not thinking about defeat. She had nothing to lose. But those words didn't ring true for her anymore. She did have something very personal to lose.

"Good. Will you join me for dinner tonight?"

"Um…"

"Not to discuss anything about Vallerio Incorporated. As a date."

"I don't think it's a good idea for us to be dating."

"Too bad. I don't care what other people think and you didn't strike me as the kind of woman who'd let that stop her either."

"I'm not going to go out with you because you dared me to."

"You're not? What would it take?" he asked.

The sincerity in his voice made her stop walking and all she could was look up at him. "I guess if you promised we'd go somewhere private, then I'd say yes."

"Consider it done. I'll pick you up at the hotel—"

She shook her head. "That won't work. I know we aren't teenagers and sneaking around might not be what you want."

"I like it," he said. "Right now being seen in public isn't in our best interest, for either of us. Tell me what you had in mind."

"I'll meet you in front of Duomo and we can go wherever you have planned."

"Okay. Be there at nine," he said. "Dress casual."

"Fine," she said, taking a step away from him. But his hand on the back of her neck stopped her. It was a light touch, a casual caress, but she shivered from it.

"If our families weren't waiting behind that glass door," he said softly, "I'd take you in my arms and kiss you again."

"I might let you," she said, just to let him know she wasn't passive. She walked away, anticipating the coming night as she'd looked forward to nothing else in the last few years.

Antonio stood to the back of the group as Dom led the tour through the factory. He'd heard the stories before and seen the model of the car they were already producing a million times before. This car—the Vallerio Roadster—was the cornerstone of the Moretti plan to retake their place in the car-making world.

He was more interested in planning his total conquest of Nathalie. He knew he'd made a lot of headway this afternoon in breaking down barriers between them. Tonight he'd do the rest of what he needed to.

He felt a twinge of something that might be guilt as he thought about using her, but it was the only way he knew how to take control of his feelings for her. He had to make their relationship about the Moretti-Vallerio feud. Otherwise he'd never be able to keep himself on track.

And that was the one thing he had to do.

He wasn't about to let all of the work he, Marco and Dom had done go by the wayside because of a woman. No matter how pretty she was. Or how much he liked her smile or even sparring with her in the boardroom. He and his brothers were the Morettis that would set the world on fire.

That wasn't going to be easy to do if he was lusting after a Vallerio.

While the Vallerio family congregated around the model car and Genevieve got behind the wheel, Dom came over to him. "What were you two doing locked in the conference room?"

"Do you have a life outside of following me around?"

"No, I don't. Moretti Motors is my life."

Antonio clapped his brother on his shoulder. "It's mine too."

Dom looked him in the eye, his hard stare very reminiscent of their grandfather's. "Good. I'm not sure what the Vallerio family is up to, but Emile is sitting on something big. He sounded very smug when we talked earlier."

"Maybe it's just his French attitude."

"Or maybe he's a bastard."

"Dom. We have to work with them. *Nono* messed around with a woman in their family. How would you feel if the situation were reversed?"

"I'd be out for blood."

"Exactly my point. Having Nathalie do the negotiation was probably the best thing Emile could do. I know that we will come to some sort of arrangement that works for all of us."

"I wanted to give you more time alone, but—"

Antonio shook his head. "We will probably do the next phase of the negotiations via e-mail. I think you and I need to show them that they can't walk away from this deal. I've given in on a few things, but they want the moon."

"This car should make them want it."

"I know that and you know that, but now we need to show them why," Antonio said. Dom was a first-class salesman and if he could genuinely talk to the

Vallerio family, Antonio knew he could win them over. And that really was the first step, because until they wanted to be a part of the new roadster they weren't going to give in. They weren't going to be willing to let Nathalie truly bargain with him. Without that, the Vallerio was never going to be more than a pipe dream.

"Why is there only a V on the hood and not the signature lion's head emblem that Pierre-Henri used on his racing uniform?" Emile asked.

"We don't have rights to that," Dom said. "We wanted to use it and incorporate as much of the Vallerio legacy as we could, but we only own the rights to this new V we've created."

"Well, if we are even going to be serious about talking of using my father's name, you are going to have to use the lion's head."

"Perfect," Antonio said. "I've asked Nathalie to go back to your board and send us an e-mail of the things you want. She knows how far we are able to go on some issues."

Emile glanced at his daughter. *"Tres bien."* Then he turned back to Dom. "I'm interested in seeing the rest of the factory. No sense in not knowing everything we'd be getting involved in."

"We do have some proprietary areas that I'm afraid we can't show you," Dom said, moving to the front of the group. "But given our shared past in F1 racing, I think you'll want to see this next area."

Dom led the way into the showcase area for their F1 program. The open-wheel car that Marco had driven the last season in his final victory was on display there. On the wall were photos of his brother in Victory Circle, and Antonio felt a rush of pride as he looked at Marco. Their younger brother was really dynamite behind the wheel. When they had been younger and talking about who would do what in Moretti Motors when they grew up, they all knew that Marco would be the face of Moretti. He craved speed the way Antonio craved winning and the way that Dom craved power.

Everyone walked around the car, which was polished to perfection and looked showroom perfect. But Antonio smelled the oil and tire rubber that had been in the air in Sao Paulo, Brazil, when Marco had become the winningest driver in Grand Prix history.

"Will you be running the Vallerio Roadster in any rally races?" Emile asked.

"That is our hope. We'd like to use it at the 24 hours of Le Mans," Dom said.

Emile stepped forward and ran his hand along the edge of the racing car. Antonio wondered if the other man had ever wanted to be a driver like Pierre-Henri.

From his own perspective he knew that not everyone inherited the desire to drive at top speeds.

"This is a fine machine. Even my father could never find fault with your F1 program."

"That is at the root of our company and something vital to Moretti Motors. We will always preserve this first, which is the main reason we are reissuing the Vallerio Roadster. We want to pay tribute to those who helped build the Moretti name to the heights it once enjoyed and will enjoy again."

"We want the same thing for the Vallerio name. My father shouldn't drop into obscurity," Emile said.

"If you are reasonable," Antonio said, "I'm sure that we will be able to come to an acceptable arrangement."

Nathalie convinced her father and sister that she needed time alone that evening to think over the proposal that Antonio had outlined. In truth she'd already made notes and recommendations to the board of the directors and had an e-mail ready to send to them in the morning. Feeling very much like a teenager, she got dressed and snuck out of the hotel to meet Antonio.

She wore a pair of slim-fitting jeans and a button-down white blouse that made her feel very American. She draped one of her favorite scarves over her head and took the stairs instead of the lift to the first floor.

Instead of hailing a cab out front, she walked the short block to the Metro station and found the proper train to Duomo.

She couldn't wait to see Antonio again. To be with him away from the pressures of their families. She rubbed the spot on her breast where Antonio had left his mark.

She felt she was doing something illicit and daring. And it was out of character for the straitlaced business-focused woman she'd always been.

She walked through the Piazza del Duomo. The crowds of people were a nice buffer and helped her to feel anonymous as she walked to the cathedral. She stood on the steps where she and Antonio had been the night before. Looking up at the wedding-cake perfection of the old stone church, she had a sense of how small her slice of time was. That her lifetime, like her grandfather's, was going to be nothing more than a wrinkle in time. Legacies, especially one like this, were all that they'd have.

She realized she was going to do whatever she could to make sure that her father and the rest of the board came to an agreement with Moretti Motors. Sure, she wanted to win and it would be nice to get this deal sealed. But she also wanted her grandfather to be remembered for generations to come. She wanted the car named after him to be talked about the way the Shelby Cobra was to muscle-heads of the world.

"Are you ready?"

He'd come up behind her, startling her.

"*Oui.* I wasn't sure where to meet you. Am I dressed okay?"

Antonio took her hand in his and led the way through the crowded piazza to a stand where motorcycles were parked. "You look perfect as always."

"Flattering me won't win you any points," she said.

"Why not?"

She studied him for a moment. He wore casual jeans and a cashmere sweater. His hair was perfectly styled and his Italian leather boots were shined. The bike he stood next to was slim and sleek. "Because I don't like lies, even the social kind, and I am very aware of what I look like in the mirror."

He opened up the seat and took out a helmet, handing it to her. "You will never convince me you don't know you are a beautiful woman."

She shook her head. "Beauty is in the eye of the beholder and I know that emotions can make a man see a woman in a different light, but you don't feel anything for me, Antonio."

"What makes you so sure?"

"Do you?" she asked, because she was fairly confident he was still playing a game with her. A game he was desperate to win. After seeing the Moretti show-room and the hall of trophies, she understood why succeeding was important to him, but she still didn't know exactly how she personally figured into his plans.

He set his helmet on the seat of the bike and then took the one from her hands. "Yes, I feel something for you. Didn't this afternoon prove that?"

"Ah, lust."

He laughed. "Women always treat that emotion with disdain, but it's very important to the mating ritual."

Mating ritual. Was he thinking of his time with her as more than just an affair? Or was he simply trying to throw her off her guard?

"Stop thinking so much, *cara mia*. Let's enjoy the night and the time that we have together."

"Where are we going?"

"To Lake Como. I have my yacht waiting for us."

"Isn't that a bit far for dinner?"

"Not at all. I wanted the evening with you and I want privacy. We won't have that here in Milan."

Still, driving two hours to the deepest lake in Italy didn't sound practical. But Antonio wasn't trying for practical. This was romance, she realized, looking into his dark blue eyes. He was going to a lot of trou-ble to seduce her; the least she could do was enjoy it.

"Fine," she said. "I've never ridden on a motor-bike before."

"I promise you are in good hands."

She sensed that she was.

He put the helmet on her head and pulled her hair free of the back. There was a sincerity and a caring to all of Antonio's moves that made her realize that he was thinking about her. Not about the Moretti-Vallerio feud or the deal that each was fighting tooth and nail to win at the other's expense.

"Is this okay?" he asked. "We can go to my place and pick up my car. But I thought this mode of transportation was more autonomous."

"It's fine. I think. I mean I've never ridden on anything without doors before."

"You'll enjoy it, *cara mia*. Riding on the bike is a sensuous feast."

She believed him. And when he helped her onto the bike and then put his own helmet on and climbed on in front of her, she realized how intimate the ride was going to be.

"Put your arms around me," he said, but she heard it close to her ear in the helmet. His voice was strong and deep and sent a sensual shiver through her.

She scooted forward and wrapped her arms around his lean waist. He put his hand over hers for a moment and then the bike roared to life as he started it. The machine vibrated between her legs and Antonio pressed against her breasts.

This was going to be the most sensual night of her life. For once she was going to forget about being a Vallerio and just enjoy being a woman.

Six

His family had had a home on Lake Como for as long as Antonio could remember. Lake Como was a jewel-like oasis of tranquility, a magical combination of lush Mediterranean foliage and snowy alpine peaks. It was one of the most beautiful spots in Italy and Antonio always felt more at peace as soon as he came out here.

He also remembered the five long years when they had to rent it out instead of coming here in the summers because money had been tight. All of that had changed as soon as Dominic, Marco and he had taken over Moretti Motors and rebuilt the family fortune in the last five years. It was that knowledge—the fact that his family had been so close to losing all of their legacy—that really drove him and his brothers.

He liked the way Nathalie felt pressed against his back as they drove through the winding streets toward Lake Como. Feeling her against him immediately brought back his arousal from earlier that afternoon.

He wanted her. No mistake about it. And he was past debating whether that desire had anything to do with Moretti Motors. He was going to be as fair as he could be with the Vallerio family. Not because of his interest in Nathalie but because he'd seen the pain in Emile's eyes when he'd spoken of his own father.

Antonio understood where Emile had been coming from. He knew too that pride was an important commodity. At Lorenzo's knee he'd grown up learning that the Moretti name was the most important thing that he, Antonio, had inherited.

"What did you tell your family you were doing tonight?" he asked to distract himself from the feel of her hands on his body.

"I told them I needed the night alone to prepare your terms." She hesitated, then added, "I don't want you to think that lying is a habit of mine."

"I don't," he said. He had a sense that Nathalie

was the type of woman who prided herself on doing what was necessary. He knew from his own experiences in life that sometimes meant white lies.

"You're a grown woman. I doubt your sister and your father are your keepers."

She laughed, the sounds soft and melodious in his ear. He liked riding like this. It had been a gamble to take her out of Milan where the deck was definitely stacked in his favor. But he had guessed that she needed to see more of the man he was than just the Moretti Motors company man.

He certainly wanted to see more of Nathalie. He wanted to see the part of her that wasn't tied to Vallerio Inc.

"My father still thinks of us as his little girls when we are in a situation like this. And he feels so tied to the Moretti Motors issue that he can't let me handle it."

"I can understand that."

"I bet you can't. Isn't it different for men? I mean your parents don't treat you like a boy, do they?"

He thought about that for a moment. His mother always did things for him that she'd done when he was little. Silly things like making sure his favorite soft drink was stocked in the house and sending him her lasagna for dinner once a week…

"I think it's different. My brothers and I are more interested in business than our father was, but I know

he worries when we travel a lot. And my mother…
well, she just mothers us."

Nathalie stroked her hand down his chest, resting
her hand on his thigh. "It is different. My dad thinks
I'm twelve."

Antonio laughed, taking her hand in his. "You
are definitely not twelve."

"Definitely."

He noticed she'd neatly turned the subject away
from business, which suited him. The last thing he
wanted to do was have Moretti Motors be between
them tonight. He wanted them to just be Antonio and
Nathalie.

Two lovers who were enjoying the romance of
this beautiful spring evening in the countryside.

"What are you thinking?" she asked.

He shrugged and turned off the motorway and
onto a small road that curved around the lake to
where his family's summer home was.

"That I'm glad you took a chance on me tonight."

"Is that what I'm doing?"

"Aren't you?" he asked, very aware that Nathalie
could be playing a game with him. Hell, she probably was. All's fair, he reminded himself.

Though he had set out to seduce her with the
romance of the evening and the beauty of his home
on Lake Como, he realized that he had to be careful

not to be seduced himself, because there was something about Nathalie tonight. Maybe it was the way her curves pressed against his back and the way her arms wrapped around his chest as he maneuvered the bike through the curves and turns of the road, or maybe it was something more.

"Are we close to your house? I read somewhere…"

"What?"

"Something very silly."

"If you read it I doubt it is all that silly."

"Well, this is. I was going to say I heard that celebrities lived in the area."

The comment was out of character for the woman he'd come to know in the boardroom. "My brother is considered a celebrity in some circles."

"Dominic?"

"Marco. You must know drivers too, right? Vallerio Incorporated is still very involved in the racing world."

"That is true," she said. "We still have patents for engines and stuff that my grandfather designed."

"Stuff?"

"Yes. Where is your home?"

"Right up here," he said, turning off the road and onto the long winding driveway that led to the stone cottage. He pulled to a stop next to the house and turned off the bike.

He removed his helmet and took Nathalie's from her when she did the same. He hung them both off the handlebars of the motorcycle and then got off the bike.

He held his hand out to her. She took it and slowly dismounted, losing her balance when she stepped off and falling right into his arms.

He only hoped she'd fall as easily into his arms later tonight.

Nathalie tried to pretend this was nothing new to her, that being on a private yacht in the middle of the very romantic Lake Como was like every other date she'd been on, but in her heart of hearts she knew it wasn't.

It had little to do with the yacht or the setting and everything to do with the man who was with her. Antonio hadn't brought up business since they'd set foot in his home. And clearly this was his home. He pointed out the home his parents owned and the ones that were his brothers'.

But he didn't focus too much on anything that wasn't personal. "Where did your family go on holiday?"

She tried to recall. She didn't dwell in the past and she'd attended a year-round boarding school with Genevieve. "We have a flat in London and my grand-parents have a house in Monte Carlo. And we had holidays in London growing up. But otherwise we didn't really go anywhere. Except I had a pen pal in Cairo when I was a girl and I visited her one time."

"What about as an adult? Where is your favorite place to go on holiday?"

"I don't take them."

"How very American of you," Antonio said.

"It's not that…. You know how earlier I said my father still thinks I'm a girl?"

"Yes."

"I still feel like I'm proving myself to him and to the board."

Antonio handed her a pomegranate martini. They were anchored in the middle of the lake, music played through the speakers and a small table had been set on the deck of the yacht. There were lights draped from the mast.

"I can understand that. I think I've been trying to prove myself for most of my career."

"To whom?" she asked. "You said your father wasn't interested in business."

"Lorenzo. Dom, Marco and I made a promise to each other that we'd be the generation to get back the promise and the fortune that Lorenzo had made."

That made sense. It also explained why they'd come to Vallerio Inc. for permission to use the Vallerio name.

"Isn't it odd that no matter how old we get we are still trying to prove something to our elders?"

"Not necessarily odd," Antonio said. "I think we are both tied so much to our families that failure is simply not an option."

She smiled at him. "Maybe that is why we are both used to winning."

"Probably. But that doesn't matter tonight. I want this evening for us."

"You've said that a couple of times. I'm not thinking about work with the moon shining down on us."

He smiled over at her. "*Buon.* Are you hungry yet?"

She shook her head. She didn't want to eat right now. She could eat any time, but this moment with Antonio wasn't going to last forever.

"Dance with me?"

"Yes." She set her martini glass down. The music was slow and bluesy. A pure American sound that sounded familiar to her but she was unable to identify the artist. She soon stopped trying when Antonio drew her into his arms.

He put one arm around her waist, drawing her as close as he could, while the music slowed its pace. His hips moved in time with the drumbeat and hers soon did the same. She wrapped her arms around his shoulders as she'd wanted to do since they'd gotten off that motorcycle of his. She had been invigorated by the ride out here, and more than ever craved his solid body pressed to hers.

The passionate encounter they'd had in the boardroom that afternoon had whet her appetite for him. And now she wanted more.

He kept his other arm in the middle of her back, stroking her spine as he danced her around the deck of the yacht. He sang softly under his breath and she thought she felt herself falling for him.

Maybe it was the magic of this night or the fact that she'd spent all day battling more with her own family than him, but at this moment she realized there was something likeable about Antonio.

His hands skirted along her sides and around to her front. "You have the sexiest body."

"Thank you," she said with a confidence that she was definitely starting to feel with this man.

"You don't give an inch, do you?"

"Do you?" she asked.

"Never."

They were perfectly suited, she thought. Perfectly suited for not only the negotiations they were brokering but also a love affair.

"Antonio?"

"*Sí?*"

"I want more than this dance with you," she said, taking the bull by the horns. Neither of them would be satisfied with anything less than this.

"Me too. I want this evening and many more, *cara mia*."

"Am I really yours?"

He tipped his head to the side to look down at her. It was hard to see his expression in the dim light, but when he spoke she heard his confidence and the sincerity in his voice.

"You will be."

She stood on her tiptoes and met his mouth as it descended toward hers. Their lips met and she darted her tongue out to taste his, but he opened his lips and sucked her tongue deep inside his mouth. Both of his arms wrapped around her, making her feel she'd found in his arms the one place she'd always searched for.

They ate a light supper and then he drew Nathalie to the aft of the yacht where he'd had his staff arrange large soft pillows for them to lie on. The staff had followed his instructions exactly.

He left her standing by the bow to go and change the music on his iPod/Bose system.

Soon soft music filled the air. The breeze was cool but not cold, and to be honest Antonio couldn't remember the last time he'd enjoyed an evening with a woman so much. And they hadn't even had sex, he thought.

"*Merci*, Antonio."

"For what?" he asked. He loved the soft sound of her voice. But mostly he loved the feel of her in his arms. He pulled her back into his arms, dancing her around the deck.

"For this evening. I really enjoyed it."

"It's not over yet."

"Good," she said.

He caressed her back and she shifted in his arms. Blood rushed through his veins, pooling in his groin as she turned in his arms and smiled up at him. An expression of intent spread over her face.

He led her over to the pillows and drew her down to them. He lay back against them and drew her into his arms. She curled against his side, her head resting on his shoulder and her arm around his waist. He stroked her arm.

"Climb up here," he said, gesturing to his lap.

"Not yet."

He arched one eyebrow at her. "Do you have something else in mind?"

"Yes," she said. "Take off your shirt."

He arched one eyebrow at her but sat up and did as she asked. "Now you do the same."

She shook her head. "I'm going to be in charge."

He captured both of her hands and turned so that she was under him. "I don't think so."

He held both of her hands loosely in one of his and undid her white blouse with the other one. Once it was unbuttoned, he let go of her hands and drew the blouse off her body.

The bra she wore was creamy white lace and afforded only partial coverage. He could see the pink color of her nipples through the pattern on her bra.

"Now you can do as you wish," he said, trying to pretend he wasn't her slave at this moment. He might want to believe he was in charge, but he knew he wasn't.

He growled deep in his throat when she brushed kisses against his chest. Her lips were sweet and bold as she explored his torso, then nibbled their way down his body.

He watched her, loving the feel of her cool hair against his heated skin. His pants felt damned uncomfortable. When her tongue darted out and brushed against his nipple, he arched off the pillows and put his hand on the back of her head, urging her to stay where she was.

Still, she eased her way down his chest. She traced each of the muscles that ribbed his abdomen and then slowly made her way lower. He could feel his heartbeat in his erection and he knew he was going to lose it if he didn't take control.

But another part of him wanted to just sit back and let her have her way with him. When she reached the edge of his pants, she stopped and glanced up to his face.

Her hand brushed over his erection. "Did you like that?"

"Sì, cara mia," he said, pulling her to him. He lifted her slightly so that her lace-covered nipples brushed his chest.

"Let's see what you like," he said.

She suddenly diverted her gaze and nibbled her lips, and he realized she didn't want to let him see what made her vulnerable. Moments before, he had no problems with letting Nathalie know exactly how much her body and her touch turned him on.

He told her so, in softly whispered words. He buried his face against her neck and drew her body close to his until she was pressed to him, tucked tightly to him.

He skimmed his hands all over her body, up and down her back, unclasping her bra and pulling it down her arms and tossing it away.

"I like the feel of your chest against me," she said.

Blood roared in his ears. He was so hard right now that he needed to be inside her.

But he took his time making love to her. Slowly he unbuttoned her jeans and drew them down her legs. They were long and lean and so soft to his touch. He pushed the fabric aside and then sat on his heels near her feet and just looked at her.

She lay back against the multicolored pillows. Clad only in a pair of pink panties, she was exquisitely beautiful and he was glad that he was the man who would claim her tonight.

He caressed her creamy thighs. *Dio,* she was soft and so responsive. It was as if she were made to be his. They were equals in other areas of life, so he shouldn't have been surprised that they were here as well.

She moaned as he neared her center and then sighed when he brushed his fingertips across the crotch of her panties. When her long legs shifted and opened, he moved between them, keeping his eyes on her.

The cotton was warm and wet. He slipped one finger under the material and hesitated for a second, looking down into her eyes.

Her eyes were heavy lidded. She bit down on her lower lip and he felt the minute movements of her hips as she tried to move his touch where she needed it.

He wasn't done teasing her or himself with the building passion between them. He nudged her panties aside and teased her opening. Tracing with his fingers, feeling the humid warmth of her body spilling out, beckoning him to come deeper. He teased her with just the tip of his finger, and she moaned and reached down to grasp his shoulders.

"What are you feeling?" he asked in Italian, needing to know.

"I can't translate Italian now," she said breathlessly.

He laughed. She'd brought him down to the very base of the man he was. He'd forgotten to speak English, which they'd almost used exclusively in their conversations. "Pardon me. You go to my head."

"Good." She squirmed against him.

He kissed her, and her mouth opened under his, her tongue tangling with his. He was so hard right now he thought he'd come in his pants. She was pure feminine temptation and he had her in his arms.

He nibbled on her and held her at his mercy as his fingers continued to tease between her legs. Her nails dug into his shoulders and she arched into him.

He rolled over so that he was under her. He stroked her back and spine, scraping his nail down the length of it. He followed the line of her back down the indentation above her backside.

She closed her eyes and held her breath as he fondled her. A sweet sound escaped her lips before he captured them. She tipped her head to the side, allowing him access to her mouth. She held his shoulders and moved on him, rubbing her body over his erection.

He shifted her back a little bit so he could see her face and watch her expression. Her breasts were bare, nipples distended and begging for his mouth. He lowered his head and suckled.

He buried his hand in her hair and arched her over his arm. Both of her breasts were thrust up at him. He had a lap full of woman and he knew that he wanted Nathalie more than he'd wanted any woman in a long time.

He realized that he wanted to erase all other men from her memory. Whatever lovers she had in the past he wanted to ensure she never recalled again. That when she thought of sharing her body with a man, his was the only face she saw.

Her eyes were closed, her hips moving subtly against him, and when he blew on her nipple he saw gooseflesh spread down her body.

"Nathalie?"

"*Oui,* Antonio?" Her voice was husky and her words spaced out. And he loved it. Loved the way she reacted to him.

"You're mine," he said.

He kept his attention on her breasts. Her nipples were so sensitive he was pretty sure he could bring her to an orgasm just from touching her there.

The globes of her breasts were full and fleshy, more than a handful. He licked the valley between her breasts. She tasted sweet and a bit salty. And like nothing he'd tasted before.

He kept kissing and rubbing until her hands clenched in his hair and she rocked her hips harder against his length. He lifted his hips, thrusting up against her. He sucked hard on her tender, aroused nipple. "Come for me, *cara mia.*"

But she braced her hands on his shoulders and pulled her body away from his. "I don't want this to just be about me."

"It won't be. I want you to come for me, Nathalie, and then we can come together."

"Promise?"

"Yes."

She lowered her body to his again and he rebuilt her passion, aroused her with all the skill he'd learned since he'd had his first woman years ago. He was glad for the knowledge gained from his past lovers because he needed to do so much more than just please Nathalie.

When he felt her hips moving against him, he caressed her feminine mound and then slowly entered her with one finger and then two. She moaned his name as he teased her. He couldn't help but smile as he continued to draw the reaction he wanted from her. He kept touching her and whispering words of sex against her, telling her what he wanted and how to give it to him.

She gasped and he felt her body tighten around his fingers as her orgasm rolled over her until she collapsed in his arms, falling down on his chest.

A moment later he set about arousing her again. He held her close, enjoying the feel of her rapid breath against his neck. The creamy moisture at the apex of her thighs told him that he'd done a good job of bringing her pleasure.

He glanced down at her and saw she was watching him. The fire in her eyes made his entire body tight with anticipation.

"I want you inside me this time, Antonio," she said, no shadows in her eyes now. "I really want you. Come to me now."

Shifting off him, she settled next to him on the pillows. She opened her arms and her legs, inviting him into her body, and he went. He took his pants off, tossing them on the deck next to her shirt and jeans. Then he lowered himself over her and caressed every part of her.

She reached between his legs and fondled his sex, cupping him in her hands, and he shuddered. He needed to be inside her now. But he had to take care of a condom first. He fumbled in his pants pocket and pulled out the condom he'd optimistically put there earlier. He sheathed himself quickly, before coming back between her legs. He shifted and lifted her thighs, wrapping her legs around his waist. Her hands fluttered between them and their eyes met.

Mine, he thought.

He held her hips steady, entered her slowly, then thrust deeply until he was fully seated. Her eyes widened with each inch he gave her. She clutched at his hips as he started thrusting, holding him to her, her eyes half closed and her head tipped back.

He leaned down and caught one of her nipples in his teeth, scraping very gently. She started to tighten around him. Her hips moved faster, demanding more, but he kept the pace slow, steady. He wanted her to come again before he did.

He suckled her nipple and rotated his hips to catch her pleasure point with each thrust and he felt her hands clench in his hair as she threw her head back and a climax ripped through her.

He varied his thrusts, finding a rhythm that would draw out the tension at the base of his spine. Something that would make his time in her body, wrapped in her silky limbs, last forever.

Leaning back on his haunches, he tipped her hips up to give him deeper access to her body. Then she scraped her nails down his back, clutched his buttocks and drew him in. His blood roared in his ears as he felt everything in his world center to this one woman.

He held her in his arms afterward, neither of them saying anything, and he feared that was because both of them knew that this had changed the stakes in their friendly little game. The family feud that had started with her great-aunt and his grandfather couldn't be continued with their generation.

Seven

Back in Paris, life seemed too hectic. Her father and sister had gone back to their lives and now that she was home Nathalie thought that Antonio and the night they'd spent together would seem less intense, but it wasn't. She had been working day and night not just on the Moretti Motors negotiations but also on the other work that crossed her desk.

Her parents had invited her to dinner tonight and she'd tried to turn them down, but Nathalie never could disappoint her mother.

It was the same with Genevieve. Maybe it was because they'd grown up closer to their mother than their father. Whatever the reason, she admitted as she drove her Peugeot on the roundabout in front of the Arc de Triomphe, she didn't care. She wanted to get through dinner as quickly as she could and then get back to work.

It was the only way she'd found to keep her mind off of Antonio. When she was at home in her luxurious condo, all she did was imagine him there with her. When she slept he haunted her dreams, making love to her and speaking to her in that beautiful Italian voice of his. When she worked out at the gym, she sometimes thought she heard his footfalls on the treadmill next to hers.

He was haunting her. Damn him.

In the office he'd sent her a very official-sounding e-mail telling her that he looked forward to hearing from her on the Vallerio Roadster matter.

And then at home she'd received a vase of yellow daffodils, which were still on her front hall table. They were the first things she saw when she came home and the last things she noticed when she left. The note he'd sent was sweet and sexy. Everything she'd expect from Antonio.

And a part of her…okay, all of her hoped that this relationship was more than an affair. But she was afraid to believe it.

He had said that they should keep their dating

private and that it had nothing to do with the negotiations they were both embroiled in right now, but
she worried that she wouldn't be able to.

Her mobile rang as she approached the restaurant and pulled into the valet lane. She glanced
down at the caller ID and saw that it was an Italian
number. Antonio?

She hurried out of her car and into Ladurée. The
restaurant was over a century old and a famous in-
stitution on the Champs-Elysées.

"Bonjour, c'est Nathalie," she said, answering
her phone.

"Ciao, cara mia. Did you get the flowers I sent?"

"Yes, I did. Thank you for them."

"You're welcome. What are you doing?"

"Having dinner with my family. I'm sorry I
haven't sent you a thank-you note."

"That's nothing. Why haven't you returned my
calls?" he asked.

She shrugged and then realized he couldn't see
that response. "I'm not sure. I've been busy."

She realized she was making excuses and she
knew better than that. "I guess I wanted a chance to
get you out of my head."

"Did it work?" he asked.

"No. Not at all."

"Well, then you should have called me back. I've missed the sound of your voice."

"Have you?"

"Indeed. When will you be back in Milan?"

"Next week. I'm meeting with our board tomorrow and I should have a counteroffer for you."

"You know how far I'm willing to go," he said.

She wondered if she really did know. How far was Antonio willing to go to get the deal closed? Was he willing to seduce her?

She didn't know. She doubted seducing her would be of benefit for him.

"Why so silent?"

"I'm just thinking," she said. She was dreaming of this man who was her rival. This man who wanted something from her family that they had fought to hold on to. And she was going to try to find a way to make it work for him. Because she wanted to honor her grandfather's memory, but also because she wanted to get this deal off the table so she could see what lay between them.

"Nathalie?"

"Um...pardon me. I've got to go. My parents are waiting."

"Call me when you are done with dinner," he said.

"It will be late."

"That's okay, I'll be up."

She hesitated. But then she thought, why the hell not? She'd be thinking about him anyway.

"All right. I'll call. I only have your office number."

"I'll send you a text with all my numbers. I'll be at home after ten."

"Very well. *Bonne nuit,* Antonio."

"Until later."

He disconnected the call and she held on to her BlackBerry for another minute, standing in the crowded foyer of the restaurant trying to regain her equilibrium.

"Nathalie!"

She turned to see Genevieve waving at her. She made her way over to her sister and hugged her. "Are Mom and Dad here?"

"Not yet. I told them we'd meet them in the bar," Genevieve said, leading the way to the bar. They both ordered a glass of wine and found a seat at one of the high tables.

"What happened that last night in Milan?"

"What? Nothing. I told you I stayed in," she said.

"I followed you to Duomo and saw you leave with Antonio."

"Busted?"

"Big-time. So what's up?"

"I…I don't know. It really has nothing to do with the negotiations."

"How can you say that? He's a Moretti. Lorenzo already proved that the men in that family are all about business."

Nathalie took a sip of her drink. "I know. But Antonio is different."

"Is he really?"

"Yes, I think he is. I know that I might be making a mistake, but I think I can handle him in the boardroom and out."

"I hope you are right," Genevieve said.

Nathalie did too. And she knew no matter what, she had to be very careful that she didn't forget that with Moretti men, business always came first.

Antonio strolled down the hall to Dominic's office. Angelina was sitting at her desk despite the fact that it was well past five.

"*Ciao,* Antonio," she said.

"*Ciao,* Angelina. Is my brother available?"

"*Sì.* Marco has just gone in."

"*Grazie.*"

He entered the office and closed the heavy oak door behind him. Marco looked relaxed and happy, despite the fact that it was the beginning of the F1 World Championship race calendar. "*Ciao,* Marco. Congratulations on your win in Behrain last weekend."

He smiled. "*Grazie*. Everyone is gunning for me this year."

"I would imagine so," Dom said.

"How is Virginia and little Enzo?"

"Very good. We'd love it if you'd join us for dinner tonight."

He nodded.

"If that's settled, can we get down to business?" Dom said.

Antonio sat in the other guest chair, listening with half an ear as Dom caught Marco up on everything that had been happening the last two weeks while he'd been out of town.

He studied his younger brother and realized, for the first time since Marco had fallen in love with Virginia, that he envied his brother. Which was ridiculous. He was a bachelor. He loved his single life, yet a part of him wanted someone to come home to. Wanted a partner that would always be there for him.

He rubbed the back of his neck, knowing that he wasn't going to find that with Nathalie. He couldn't. No matter how much he wanted her in his life, his priority had to always be Moretti Motors.

"Tony?"

"Hmm?"

"Did you hear what I said?" Dom asked. "The leak is in the corporate offices. I've asked Ian to meet us after the dinner hour tonight. He has some information that he didn't want to give to me at the office."

"I don't like the sound of that," Antonio said. "He must think that the problem is in one of our offices."

"I'm not going to guess at anything. Can you join us after dinner?"

He thought about the call he'd coerced Nathalie into making. He wanted to talk to her, but canceling an important meeting for her… Well, that would be giving her too much power in his personal life and he wasn't willing to do that just now. "*Sì*, I'm available."

"*Buon.* So, where do we stand on the Vallerio negotiations?"

"I offered them a share of the profits from the roadster, and a seat on the board for the CEO of Vallerio Incorporated. They want to do profit sharing companywide for all of their shareholders. I've told them we'll consider it if it's a reciprocal arrangement."

"Is that fiscally a good idea?" Dom asked.

"I am doing some research on their profit and loss statements for the last couple of years. They are expecting a huge profit in the third quarter this year, but I haven't been able to figure out why."

"Doesn't Nathalie know?" Dom asked.

"I'm sure she does but I haven't asked her yet. She

is busy with figuring out what her board will accept and preparing a counteroffer."

"I thought you were working on seducing her to get more information," Dom said.

"It's never that easy with women," Marco said. "You must know that, Dom."

"Indeed, but this time I think it's important that Tony pull out all the stops."

"Are you giving him romantic advice?" Marco asked. "What have you two been up to while I've been racing?"

Antonio knew this was going to continue going downhill. Marco would tease him endlessly because Dom had suggested he seduce Nathalie. Antonio realized that to anyone on the outside the ploy was going to seem cold and calculated.

Still, Antonio knew he hadn't seduced her for any reason other than that he wanted her. He was attracted to her body and soul, he thought.

"Tony?"

"Dom suggested I use sex as another means of weakening her defenses."

"Did you? That's ethically wrong," Marco said.

"Of course it is. Nathalie and I are both very aware of our family rivalry," Antonio said.

"That's good. Do you like her?" Marco asked.

He shrugged. No way was he going to talk about

Nathalie with his brothers. Dom would find it uncomfortable if he mentioned that he was attracted to Nathalie in a way he'd never been attracted to another woman. And he knew that he didn't want to have to choose between his loyalty to his brothers and to Nathalie.

Was he loyal to her? He didn't like to think that she had any control over him, but he knew she did.

"Of course I like her. She's sexy and smart, a lethal combination in any woman."

Marco laughed and Dom looked uncomfortable. "Can you handle her?"

"She's only a woman," Antonio said. Now if he could only convince his emotions of that fact.

Nathalie waved her mother and sister off as they went to the bakery section of the restaurant to buy something yummy for all of them. Her father was going to ride back to her parents' house with her. He wanted, as he'd said, to make sure she still realized that the Vallerio family had been done a grave injustice.

The valet brought her car and she got in after tipping the man. Her father sat quietly until she'd navigated out of the traffic on the Champs-Elysées.

"Thank you for all your hard work with the Moretti Motors people," Emile said, "but I don't think this newest offer of theirs is going to be one we can accept."

"Why not? I think the terms are good and that we will make the profit that we wanted to from this agreement."

Nathalie made a left turn and then glanced over at her father. His mouth was pinched tight and he looked like a very old man for a minute. "Papa?"

"I'm fine. We don't need the Morettis to make a profit. I don't want to give away the farm just to have a piece of their pie."

She shook her head. "I know what I'm doing."

"Do you? I've always been impressed by your business savvy and the way you conduct yourself, but Antonio Moretti…he's slick and smooth and I'm not sure you can handle him."

If her father only knew. She'd faced men like Antonio on more than one occasion and always come back a winner. "Papa, don't you trust me?"

"*Oui, cherie,* I trust you."

"Then why are you asking me all these questions?"

"I guess it is simply that I don't trust the Moretti men not to do something underhanded. And you are my daughter, Nathalie. I don't want you hurt the way my aunt Anna was."

She understood that. "I'm not *Tante* Anna, Papa, and I'm not going to let Antonio use me the way that Lorenzo did her. I'm more than capable of handling myself around Antonio."

"*Bien.* That's all I wanted to say. Also we cannot accept less than seventy percent of the profits from the roadster. I talked to the rest of the board already and they are adamant as well."

Nathalie turned onto the street where her parents lived. "Papa, that's impossible. Antonio has already turned that offer down."

"Then tell him he'll have to try harder to come up with a better offer than he has so far."

"I will."

Nathalie parked on the street in front of her parents' house with a feeling that her father was never going to accept any relationship she had with Antonio. And that made her a little sad because she had started to see Antonio as a man. Not the Moretti monster that her family had always painted the Moretti heirs to be.

Holding his nephew reinforced to Antonio how important it was to focus on the legacy of Moretti Motors. Marco and Virginia were obviously in love and Antonio saw no latent signs of the Moretti curse in his brother's house, but as they left to go meet Ian Stark and Antonio handed his nephew back to Virginia, he realized that he didn't want to take any chances.

He didn't want Enzo to experience what he and his brothers had when their house had to be sold and they had to move to *Nono*'s house. That wasn't acceptable to him.

He knew that meant he had to cool it with Nathalie. He had to treat her the same way he would treat any other woman he'd started an affair with. Sending flowers was okay, but one-of-a-kind nightgowns probably wasn't the right tone if he wanted to keep this relationship like all of his other affairs.

But it was too late to cancel the sexy negligee he'd ordered to be delivered tomorrow morning. Earlier he'd thought he'd seduce her further over the phone and then send her that sexy nightgown for her to wear the next time she came to Milan. But now… Oh, hell, he wasn't sure.

He followed Dom to his home, which was only three streets from Marco's. They'd all purchased homes in the same area of Milan so that they were close to the Moretti Motors corporate offices and each other. They were only eighteen months apart and had always been very close.

There was a Porsche 911 in the driveway and Antonio shook his head as he got out. Only Ian would drive a rival car to Dom's house.

Luigi, Dom's butler, let him in and directed him to the den, where Ian and Dom waited for him.

"Dom, you've got a big piece of trash in front of your house," Antonio said as he entered.

"Most people don't consider a Porsche trash, Tony."

"I can't speak to others' ignorance," Antonio said.

Ian laughed and stood up to shake his hand. "Good to see you."

"You as well. So, did you find our leak?" Antonio said.

"I did. I think it's going to shock you both."

"Nothing would shock me," Dom said.

"Not even the fact that the leak is your secretary, Angelina de Luca?"

"What? Are you sure?" Dom asked. He crossed to the bar on one wall and poured two fingers of whiskey into a highball glass and swallowed it in one long draw.

"Positive. She's been feeding information to ESP Motors. I saw the last drop myself."

"What the hell?" Dom said.

Antonio was surprised and concerned. "She's had free rein of our corporate offices. She knows everything."

"I know that," Dom said.

"What should we do next?" Ian asked. "I have enough evidence to go to the police. We can have her arrested and press charges."

"Do you have enough to prove ESP was behind it?" Antonio asked. ESP was the company founded by Nigel Eastburn, Lorenzo Moretti's biggest rival on and off the racetrack. Both men had started their own car companies after retiring. The launch of the Vallerio model had pushed Lorenzo ahead of Nigel, but in the '80s when Moretti Motors had started to fail, ESP Motors, named after Nigel and his two partners Geoffrey Saxby and Emmitt Pearson, had moved ahead. And that was why Moretti Motors wanted the roadster to be a success—to take back the pride that they'd lost when ESP had become the name synonymous with roadsters.

"If you give me another week or so, I'll get the proof. I need to make sure their guy isn't working independently."

"Who is it?"

"I believe it's Barty Eastburn."

"Nigel's grandson? That is big. Well, I'd rather take him down than just Angelina."

"She can't get off with no punishment," Antonio said.

"She won't," Dom said. The fierceness of his tone made Antonio realize that Dom was furious at Angelina's betrayal.

Eight

Nathalie was no closer to figuring out anything about her relationship with Antonio when she arrived in Milan a week later. She hadn't called Antonio or spoken to him since their one conversation before her dinner.

She was trying very hard to convince herself that she was only happy to be in Milan to resolve the outstanding issues she had with Moretti Motors, but she was failing.

She wanted to see Antonio. She was a bit mad at herself that she hadn't called him back, but after her conversation with her father she'd felt it was important to keep her distance. Now as she waited in the Moretti Motors lobby she knew nothing was more important than seeing Antonio.

As soon as he stepped off the elevator and started walking toward her, she had the insane desire to run to him.

"Good afternoon, Nathalie. Welcome back to Milan," he said. He welcomed her with a kiss on each cheek.

She turned her head toward him at the last second and her lips brushed his cheek.

"It's good to be back."

"Why didn't you call me, *cara mia?*"

She held her briefcase in one hand and followed him through the hallway to the conference room. "I…I don't know. I mean I had good reasons at first, but now that I'm here they don't seem valid."

"We can discuss that later, over dinner and drinks."

"Antonio, do you think that's a good idea?"

"Yes, I do. Did you get the gift I sent?"

"I did. I'm sorry I haven't thanked you properly." She'd put the negligee on and slept in it every night since he'd sent it. It was exquisite and since she knew the store where he'd purchased it, she also knew it was one of a kind. She'd been touched that he'd sent her the nightgown, but afraid to call him. Afraid that if she talked to him she'd forget to remain strong on the negotiations.

"You can do so later."

"Can I?" she asked, refusing to let him get away with bossing her around.

"Yes, you may," he said, with an unrepentant grin. "I've invited Dominic to join us. He has a counter-offer since we are at an impasse."

Antonio's words made her realize she needed to put all of her personal thoughts on hold and focus on this meeting. How could she tell Antonio that the Vallerio board wasn't going to be satisfied with anything less than a deal that was on their terms? She decided to be straightforward.

"I'll be happy to listen to your proposal, but I'm afraid nothing less than what we've asked for will suffice."

"Is there nothing I can do that would make them change their minds?"

She shook her head. "If you want to back down on your stance, we could move forward."

"I don't see that happening."

"So it's back to the drawing board," she said.

"Hear Dom's presentation. I think it'll make a huge difference."

"You know this isn't just about business," she said. "Almost everyone on the board is related to my grandfather and he was so angry about what Lorenzo did to Anna."

"What did he do?" Antonio asked. "Because from what we heard, she left him. Went back to Paris and never returned."

"He kicked her out, Antonio. He told her she wasn't the wife he needed to build his dynasty with."

Antonio looked over at her. "Some men don't know how to handle themselves with a woman who offers too much temptation."

"Is that a problem for you?" she asked.

"It never has been, but to be honest you do stay on my mind more than I wish you would."

"Do I?" she asked. She didn't want to talk about them, because if she weren't careful she'd fall for him—harder than she already had. It already was a very real danger because she was ready to go back to her board of directors and do whatever it took to convince them to take this deal.

"*Sì*, you do. Why is that?" he asked. He glanced at the closed boardroom door to the table and she almost blushed when she remembered what had occurred the last time they were alone in this room.

She tipped her head to one side. "Perhaps because you've met your match."

"I think I have," he said, leaning back against the

table in the exact spot where she'd sat when he'd pleasured her. "But then you must have too."

"I don't know about that. I'm more than capable of taking whatever you have to dish out."

He reached for her, his hands on her waist as he drew her closer to him. He spread his legs and less than a second later she was in his arms. Nestled there where she'd secretly wanted to be.

"This is so inappropriate for the business we are conducting."

"That might be, but I've missed you, *amore*."

She glanced at the closed door and then leaned up on her tiptoes and kissed him. For a week now she'd gone to sleep with only the remembered feel of his arms around her and his mouth pressed to hers. The reality was so much better than her memories.

She kissed him as if this was the last embrace they'd have. In a way it was. After her talk with her father she'd known that nothing lasting could come of her affair with Antonio. No matter how much she might want something more.

That evening when he picked Nathalie up, Antonio wasn't sure he was doing the right thing, but he knew that unless he got her to see his family as something more than monsters she was never going to be able to convince the Vallerio board to soften their position.

And truly the only way to do that was to let Nathalie meet his parents. His father was as different from Lorenzo as any man could be. Giovanni had filled his life with one passion and that was his wife, Philomena. Antonio knew that once Nathalie met them she'd see that the Moretti men weren't out to crush the Vallerio family once again.

He wanted to make her see that they were sincere in their offer to put Vallerio back on the lips of car connoisseurs the world over.

"Are you sure about this?" she asked once they were seated in his car.

"Positive. I had the opportunity to meet your father and sister and now I think it's time you had the same."

"Aren't they going to be angry that I haven't convinced my board to accept all of your terms?"

"No. I doubt they will say anything to you about business. My parents aren't concerned about that at all."

"What are they concerned about?"

Antonio thought about that for a moment. "Each other. And that my brothers and I are happy."

"I can't imagine that Lorenzo's son wouldn't be as passionate about car making as he was."

"Wait until you see my parents. They have a love that consumes them."

"I still don't understand," she said. "Many men are married and still manage a company."

"But those men weren't cursed to be lucky either in love or in business," Antonio said.

"And your family was?" she asked.

"Indeed. In fact your great-aunt may have fallen victim to the same curse."

"How do you figure?" she asked.

"Lorenzo broke the heart of a girl he'd left behind in his village to go and seek his fortune, and she cursed him when he didn't fulfill his promise to her."

"What promise?"

Antonio glanced away from the road and over at Nathalie. She seemed very interested in his story. And he wanted to share it. Wanted her to understand that there was more to Lorenzo than his callous behavior might have indicated. "The promise to marry her once he had won the Grand Prix championship and started his car company."

"Promises he didn't keep?"

"No. Lorenzo needed more time to make his fortune. His parents were poor farmers who never did more than eke out an existence and he wanted better for his children."

"So he asked her to wait for him, or did he send her home?" Nathalie asked.

"He told her he couldn't fulfill his promise until

he was certain he'd have the future they both wanted. He asked her to wait awhile longer. She returned home to her village and waited."

"How do you know all of this?"

"Marco's wife, Virginia, is the granddaughter of Cassia, Lorenzo's first love. She has Cassia's journal."

"She cursed your grandfather but your brother married her granddaughter?"

"That makes us sound crazy, I know, but the curse she put on Lorenzo was also put on succeeding generations. When you meet my parents you will see they have a love that is just as successful as Moretti Motors was under *Nono*'s leadership. As successful as it will be now that Marco, Dom and I are running things."

She gave him a very queer look, then turned away, glancing down at her hands, which were laced together in her lap. "Does that mean your brothers don't expect to find the love your parents have?"

Antonio tried not to think of love. It wasn't really something that he'd craved. He had his parents' love and he had never lacked for feminine company and he had his brothers. What more could a man need?

"I don't know," he said honestly. "Love… romantic love just isn't something I've ever really wanted to have."

"Why not?"

"Maybe because of how badly *Nono* screwed it up. Virginia's grandmother cursed him, hated him so much that she wanted to make sure he never felt love again. Your great-aunt hated him so much that she turned Pierre-Henri against him.

"With that kind of a legacy do you think I'd even entertain falling for a woman?"

"But your father isn't that type of man," she said.

Antonio had often thought the same thing. But he'd seen Dom crash and burn with a love affair when he was in university and Antonio had realized whether they wanted to believe in a curse or not he and his brothers had inherited *Nono*'s bad mojo when it came to love and women.

"He's also not the businessman Lorenzo was."

"I see. Since you are good at business, it follows you'll be a screwup with women."

Antonio turned on the long winding driveway that led to his parents' estate in San Giuliano Milanese. He stopped the car in the circular drive at the front of the house. "I have never been a screw-up with women. You asked about love and that's an emotion I've never really sought out."

And it had never found him, he thought. Until now. Seeing the disappointment in Nathalie's eyes, he wanted to be the man who could give her everything she wanted. Including love.

He wanted to be able to make a grand gesture as his father had when he'd walked away from Moretti Motors.

"I guess I understand what you are saying. You haven't looked for love and it hasn't found you."

"Have you?" he asked. The thought of Nathalie loving another man made a red rage fill him. He didn't want any other man to have any claim on Nathalie. And that very possessiveness bothered him as nothing else ever had.

She shook her head. "I've always been too focused on making a name for myself at Vallerio Incorporated."

Antonio's family was warm and welcoming to her. They had dinner in the garden under the stars and it didn't take her long to realize what Antonio had meant by the love his parents shared.

The men left the table to have a cigar in the lower part of the garden. Nathalie felt a moment's panic when she realized she was going to be alone with two women she had nothing in common with—Antonio's mother and his sister-in-law.

"I'm so glad you could join us tonight for dinner. The boys are so excited about their new car, and working with your family to get the Vallerio name is so important to them," Philomena said.

Antonio's mom was short, curvy and still had ebony-colored hair. She had held her own during dinner, but it had been obvious to Nathalie that she doted on the men in her life, and hearing her call Antonio and his brothers "the boys" was something that made her smile.

"Thank you for inviting me. I'm glad to see my grandfather's name being used in conjunction with a car again."

"Marco said your grandfather was pure magic when it came to open-wheel racing," Virginia said. She was a lively woman who had an aura of earthiness about her. She held her son cradled in her arms and often bent down to brush a kiss on Enzo's forehead.

Nathalie sadly had never seen her grandfather drive. She was more acquainted with the man he'd been after Lorenzo Moretti had married and divorced his sister. The man who had retreated into his workroom and focused more on what was happening under the hood. "I never got to see him drive until today."

Dom had put together a documentary that they were going to run in their suite at the F1 races for the rest of the year. The film showed Lorenzo and Pierre-Henri in their glory days. To be honest, the film had done a lot to make her look at all the Morettis in a different way. They had honored her grandfather in a way she hadn't believed they would.

She hoped even her father realized that. If he didn't, she was now determined to convince him.

Philomena's question intruded on her thoughts.

"How long will you and Marco stay in Milan?" she asked Virginia.

"Just another night. Then we are off to Barcelona for the Catalunya Grand Prix. Actually, I'm not sure if Marco mentioned this to you but we were hoping you'd babysit little Enzo here. It's our anniversary of sorts," Virginia said.

"We'd love to. You know I had a nursery prepared here as soon as we had the news of your pregnancy."

"Thank you," Virginia said.

"I've always wanted grandchildren, but I feared my boys were never going to settle down."

Nathalie understood why. "Moretti Motors is as important to them as family."

Virginia nodded. "I think sometimes that to them it *is* family and not a business at all. And of course the curse my grandmother had placed on the Morettis hung over the boys' heads."

Not a superstitious person herself, Nathalie found it hard to believe that so many of these people were. Virginia hardly seemed like a witch, but she'd told the story at dinner of how she'd used her limited knowledge of the old Strega ways to break the curse on Marco.

The curse that Cassia had placed on Lorenzo and every generation that followed.

Nathalie thought that Antonio and Dominic might believe they were still cursed. That by not finding love they hadn't found a way out of the blight that Cassia Festa had put on them. She couldn't help but sympathize with the close-knit Morettis.

"How often do you all get together?" she asked.

"Not often enough. Marco and Virginia travel most of the year for the Grand Prix. Antonio is here in Milan, but he is always busy, and Dominic goes between the offices here and the Grand Prix races."

"Do you attend the races?" Nathalie asked Philomena as they sipped coffee. Night had fallen and the sweet smell of flowers filled the air.

"Mostly the ones in Europe and always the first and last race of the season."

"You should come to the race in Barcelona next week," Virginia urged Nathalie. "There is so much excitement and energy at the races."

Nathalie doubted she would. Her father would have a fit if she attended a Grand Prix race before they had a deal with Moretti that satisfied him. "Thank you for the invitation. Is it always exciting to watch or are you ever afraid?"

Philomena blessed herself and uttered a small prayer under her breath. "I am afraid every time Marco gets in the race car. One of the Team Moretti drivers almost died last year."

Nathalie reached over and put her hand on Philomena's. "I'm sorry. I didn't mean to bring up bad memories."

"You didn't," Virginia said. "But it is a scary profession and even though I know that Marco is a very skilled driver I am reminded most weeks that this is a very dangerous profession."

Nathalie could see that. She was worried about falling in love with the son of her family's sworn enemy, but Virginia had to worry about the man she loved possibly dying. It put a lot of things in perspective for her.

She realized that she didn't want Antonio to be in danger. Then it hit her sitting her in this garden with his mother and his sister-in-law that she was in love with Antonio.

And once that realization opened her eyes, everything else fell into place. She hadn't returned to Milan to broker a deal. She'd returned to Milan to be with Antonio. In Paris it was easy to ignore the truth and to pretend that she didn't love Antonio, but tonight under the Milan moon there were no denials. Only the truth. And she was still dealing with that truth twenty minutes later when Antonio returned.

He looked at her and she could do nothing but smile at him. The man she loved.

Nine

Antonio drove to Nathalie's hotel in Milan in silence. Something was on her mind but he had no idea what. It had been a calculated move to bring her to his parents' house, and now he was wondering what the aftereffects would be. "Are you okay?"

"Yes. Dinner was very nice."

"I'm glad you enjoyed it."

"And I think I see what you meant about your parents' love. Your father is positively smitten with your mother."

"Yes, he is."

"Funny to think that a curse would have given him that much love in his life."

Antonio turned to her when he stopped for a traffic light. "I don't think he's cursed at all."

"Do you think the men in your family are? When we talked earlier I couldn't tell if you really believed you were doomed."

"Doomed to spend my life alone?" he asked. "Maybe I did. I guess that when you grow up with that kind of love in your home and then you visit with friends, you start to see that not everyone has that kind of love."

He didn't elaborate and she wanted to ask if he had wanted to find what his parents had. She knew that she and Antonio couldn't have that. She was never going to be like his mother and stay home and give up her own ambition.

She shook her head. Realizing she loved Antonio was one thing. Thinking about marriage was another. Had she lost it? Too much needed to be resolved between them businesswise before they could ever consider anything permanent. "What is it about your parents' love for each other that you really envy…I mean want?"

"I've never really thought about it," he said. He pulled into the parking area of her hotel, where the valet took the car.

She looked at him and asked, "Would you like to come up?"

"I was hoping you'd ask me. I've missed holding you."

That little confession eased the worries she had felt since she'd first realized that she loved him.

"Me too."

They walked next to each other through the lobby. In the lobby bar Antonio saw a few associates who waved him over, but he shook his head. "I don't want to talk business tonight."

"Is this going to be awkward tomorrow?" she asked when they entered the elevator alone. "This isn't the first time we've been seen together."

"I think my family knows how I feel about you. I didn't just invite you to dinner tonight as a representative of Vallerio Incorporated."

Or had he? He was a brilliant strategist and he had to know that seeing his family would make it harder for her to stand firm on what her board of directors wanted.

He had made the Morettis human to her. He had shown her the people behind the car company and that was softening her attitude toward them.

"It was nice to meet your family, but I have to wonder if you didn't plan it that way…use it as a way to soften me up," she said once they were in her suite.

"Why would I do that?" he asked. He shrugged out of his suit jacket and draped it over the back of the love seat.

"All's fair in love and in war," she said, crossing to the wet bar and taking out a bottle of mineral water. "Would you like something to drink?"

"I'll have a beer," he said.

She handed him a bottle, and he took her hand in his.

"Listen, Nathalie, I stopped trying to find an advantage to use to get you to give in a long time ago."

"Did you really?"

"Yes. I don't want you to surrender to me. I want to find a solution that will make us both happy."

"If I said that Moretti Motors should go ahead with their alternate plans you'd be fine with that?"

He took a swallow of his beer and then looked her straight in the eye. "No, I wouldn't. I think you know that. What would make me happy is coming to an arrangement that both of our boards will find pleasing."

She stepped back from him and walked to the window of her suite. "I'm…I'm confused, Antonio. For the first time in my life I can't just focus on work."

"Why is that?" he asked.

"You made me invest more of myself in this negotiation than I wanted to."

"I made you?"

She shook her head. "Not like you forced me into it...I guess I don't really mean that. I meant that I am different this time because of how I feel about you."

He put his beer on the coffee table and walked across the small room to her. He stopped when only an inch of space separated them.

He took her water from her hand and put it on the bar. "How do you feel about me, *cara mia?*"

"I..." *I love you,* she thought. But she couldn't say the words out loud. Though he'd claimed to have softened his stance on the negotiations, she couldn't hand him the powerful weapon of her love to use against her.

She shook her head. "I care about you, Antonio."

He drew her into his arms. He hugged her close to his chest and whispered soft words against her temple. She felt safer in her love with his arms around her.

Antonio claimed Nathalie's lips with his and didn't let her go until they'd reached the bed. He'd had enough talking. He was never going to be able to say the right thing to her. The thing that would make her forget that he was a Moretti and she was a Vallerio. That was always going to be between them.

Earlier tonight Dom had been very blunt that he wanted the Vallerio deal closed. He wanted Antonio to pull out all the stops. Antonio couldn't tell his brother that he wouldn't do it. That he was falling for the tall French redhead who was just as strong as he was in the boardroom and in the bedroom.

But now he was in control. And it was important to him that he make her understand this as well.

In three strides he was to the bed. He set Nathalie on her feet and peeled back the covers of the bed. He toed off his loafers and reached down to remove his socks. She still had her shoes on. He bent down and lifted her foot, carefully removing one high heel and then the other.

He stood back up. She looked exquisite in her sapphire wrap dress, like a male fantasy come to life. The neckline plunged deep between her breasts, revealing the creamy white tops of each one, while the hemline ended high on her thigh.

The only light in the room spilled from the city lights outside the window. Darkness enveloped them in a cocoon, as if no one else existed but the two of them. Antonio intended to make the most of their privacy.

He lowered his head and with his tongue, traced the edge where fabric met skin. She smelled of perfume and a natural womanly scent that he associated only with Nathalie. The scent of her skin had haunted him during the week they had been apart. Now he closed his eyes and buried his face between her breasts, inhaling deeply.

Shifting slightly to the right, he tasted her with languid strokes of his tongue. Her skin was sweeter and more addicting than anything he'd ever tasted. He followed the curve of her breast from top to bottom; the texture changed as he reached the edge of her nipple.

The velvety nub beckoned him and he pushed the fabric of her dress out of the way. He wanted to see her.

"Stand here."

He crossed the room and flipped on the light switch flooding the room in light. Nathalie stood where he left her, her red hair hanging around her shoulders in long curls. Her lips looked full and lush, wet and swollen from his kisses. Her breasts spilled from the fabric, full and white and topped with hard little berries that made his mouth water.

He crossed back to her side in less than two strides. "That's better."

"Is it?" she asked.

"I want to see you, Nathalie. The real you, not the dream that's been haunting me."

He didn't give her a chance to respond. He might be playing the fool, but right now he didn't care. He already knew he was compromised where she was concerned. She had a power over him that he could only hope she never realized she had. And he had a new goal—one that had absolutely nothing to do with Moretti Motors.

That goal was to get as deep inside her body as he could.

He lowered his head once more to the full globe of her breast, scraping the aroused nipple with his teeth. She shuddered in his arms. He used his hand to stimulate her other nipple, circling it with his finger and scraping his nail across the center very carefully while at the same time using his teeth on the first one.

She moaned his name, undulating against him. Her hands swept down his body and she unzipped his pants. His erection sprang into her waiting hands. He wanted her to grasp the length of him, but instead she only teased him by running her finger up and down the sides of his shaft.

He suckled her nipple deep in his mouth and slid his hand up under her skirt, where he encountered a sexy thong. He caressed her sticky curls through the lace, and her touch on him changed, became more fevered, more demanding.

He slipped his finger inside the crotch of her panties and into her humid opening. She moaned and lifted her leg to give him deeper access. The moan was nearly his undoing. He couldn't wait much longer to take her.

He turned and lay back on the bed, pulling Nathalie on top of him. She braced her hands on his chest and leaned up over him. Their groins pressed together. She bit her lower lip and rotated on him. It felt deliciously hot and he wanted nothing more than to let her rock against him until they both came. Later, he thought. Right now he needed to be inside her.

He pulled her down to him and rolled until she was underneath him again.

"Do you have to be on top?"

He smiled at her. "It's a male thing."

"Why?"

"Because you are too strong. I want you to know that you are ceding to my will," he said.

He didn't want to say any more, but for once he wanted to feel he was really in control. In control of their lovemaking and in control of this woman who gave away so little.

He tore his shirt off and tossed it across the room and then kicked his pants down. He reached for the bodice of Nathalie's dress and tugged until the fabric ripped, leaving her body bare.

He slid his hand down to her panties.

"Stop."

He did, glancing up at her. She reached underneath his body and pushed the panties down her legs. "I like these and don't want you to tear them."

He chuckled. "I wasn't going to rip them."

He bent his head and followed the path of her skimpy underwear with his mouth. Some of her wetness had rubbed against her thigh and he licked her clean. Then he rose over her.

He bent her legs back against her body, leaving her totally exposed to him. Leaning down, he tasted her pink flesh, caressing her carefully with his tongue until her hips were rising against him and her hands clenched in his hair. He slid up her body, holding her hips in his hands, tilting them upward to give him greater access.

He grabbed one of the pillows from the head of the bed and wedged it under her. Then draping her thighs over his arms, he brought their bodies together. Nathalie reached between them and grasped him, guiding him to her entrance.

"Take me," she said.

He did. He entered her deeply and completely, stopping only when he was fully seated within her. He felt her clench around him. He knew she was doing it intentionally and smiled down at her. He lowered his head and took her mouth, allowing his tongue to mimic the movements of his hips. Soon he felt close to the edge. It wasn't going to be much longer until he climaxed in her arms.

She rotated her hips against him with each thrust and soon she was gasping for breath and making those sweet sounds of preorgasm. He reared back, so he could go deeper, her feet on his shoulders.

He held her still for his thrusts and she tilted her head back, her eyes closing as her orgasm rushed over her. It was all he needed to send him over the edge. He felt the tingling at the base of his spine and then emptied himself into her.

Knowing she'd said too much earlier, Nathalie didn't wait for Antonio to say anything now that they were in bed. When he made love to her she felt like a woman. Not the Vallerio daughter or the Vallerio Inc. corporate shark, just a woman.

His woman.

"Do you want to see the negligee you sent me?"

"I'd love to see it," he said.

The light was still on and she went to the wardrobe where she'd hung her clothes earlier in the day. She drew out the gown.

It was a Carine Gilson gown. The exclusive lingerie couture was one of the most expensive in the world. "How did you know I like Gilson?"

"I noticed your bra the first time we made love," he said.

"Most men wouldn't have noticed."

"I'm not most men. Put on the gown. I had to rely on my imagination when I ordered it."

She did as he asked. The sheer gown fell to her knees and she stood in front of him boldly, allowing him to feast his eyes on her. The gold fabric made her skin look even creamy in the light, and the black designs on the side and at the hem added a hint of elegance.

"Come here," he beckoned from the bed. She couldn't help but notice his erection and inwardly she smiled, knowing she had the power to make him hard.

"Turn around."

She did as he said and felt his hand on her thighs, teasing up under the hem of the negligee, then caressing the crease in her buttocks. She shivered with awareness.

Reaching behind her, she found his erection and encircled it with her hand, tugging on it once and then letting go as she stepped away.

Suddenly he came up behind her, his arms coming around to grasp her breasts. He nipped at the shell of her ear. "Gotcha."

She shivered. He plucked at her aroused nipples with his fingers while his mouth continued to play at her neck. Sensation spread throughout her body.

His erection nestled between her buttocks through the fabric of her gown and she shifted a little, rubbing him between them.

One of his hands slipped down her body. He lingered at her belly button, and then slid lower, parting her nether lips. He didn't touch her, just held her open so that the fabric of her gown brushed against her clitoris. She moaned.

"Please," she gasped.

She felt like a prisoner to her desire and to this man. She tried to escape from Antonio's grip but couldn't.

He chuckled in her ear. "You're mine."

Deep in her soul, those words sounded right. She ignored that feeling and focused instead on the physical. She reached behind her to his erection, taking him in her grip. But he pulled his hips back, not allowing her to touch him.

"Antonio," she said.

"Sì, cara mia?" he asked.

"I…" She couldn't think, couldn't speak. She just wanted him inside her. Now.

"You can say it. You need me."

"I do."

"Say it please," he said. He rubbed the fleshy part of her labia with long strokes of his fingers. First one side and then the other. But she ached for more. She shifted again, trying to bring his hand where she wanted it, but he wouldn't be budged. She shoved her own hand down her body, but he caught her before she could bring relief to herself.

"Impatient?"

"You have no idea," she muttered.

He chuckled. Finally he touched her, just a light brush of his fingertip. She reached for him but again he canted his hips away from her touch. "Antonio, no more games."

"Agreed. Lie on the bed on your back."

She did. He pushed the fabric of her negligee high to her waist, parted her legs and moved between them. "Part yourself for me. Show me where you want my tongue."

She did as he said and felt his breath on her. She knew he was seeing her swollen with need and hungry for his mouth. He lowered his head and exhaled against her sensitive flesh.

Her thighs twitched and she wanted to clamp her legs around his head until he made her scream with passionate completion. She felt his tongue against her, lapping at her with increasing strength. Then she felt the edge of his teeth and she screamed with pleasure.

He thrust two fingers inside her, rocking up against her g-spot while his mouth worked its magic on her. He feathered light touches in between shockingly rougher ones that brought her quickly to the edge of orgasm. Still she fought it off, not wanting to end it too quickly.

He added a third finger inside her body and stretched them out when he pulled back and then thrust back into her body. Everything inside her tightened and her climax rushed through her.

Antonio put his hands on her thighs and pushed her legs back against her body before entering her so deeply she felt impaled on his length.

But he stopped there. She opened her eyes and met his gaze. "What are you waiting for?"

"You."

She shifted onto him. Holding his shoulders, she lifted herself off him and then slowly slid back down.

"Faster," he urged.

"Not yet," she said.

She tightened her muscles around him, milking him as she pushed herself up his length and letting him slip out of her body.

He grabbed her hips and pulled her down while he thrust upward. He worked them together until she felt every nerve ending tingling again and her second orgasm rushed over her just as Antonio screamed with his own release.

The sex was phenomenal, the best she'd ever experienced, but as he turned off the lights and took her in his arms and she relaxed against him she realized that the real power that Antonio held over her was this. The sense of rightness she felt in his arms as he held her gently and they both drifted toward sleep.

Ten

The next two weeks were the most intense of his life. Antonio felt more alive than he ever had before. He was exhausted from traveling between Milan and Paris but he thought the fatigue well worth it.

He had ensured that Nathalie and Vallerio Inc. would accept Moretti Motors latest offer. And tonight he was going to propose to Nathalie. From the conversations they'd had about love and that fairer emotion, he sensed that she was in love with him and he felt deeply pleased by that.

He couldn't admit to loving her. He was hedging his bets on the curse that had been a part of his life for so long that he couldn't just admit it. He wouldn't compromise all that he and Dom and Marco had worked for by admitting he'd fallen for Nathalie Vallerio, but he did need her in his life.

"Antonio, do you have a minute?"

He looked up from his computer screen. "Sure, Dom, come on in."

Dom came into his office and closed the door but not all the way. He stood there in the middle of the room, and for the first time Antonio saw that Dom wasn't confident. Not the way he'd always been.

"What's up?"

"Nothing really. Nothing important, I just wanted to let you know that Angelina will be continuing as my secretary."

"Are you sure that's a good idea?"

"Well, I have decided to use her to leak false information to Barty Eastburn. If he wants our company secrets, then he'll get them."

"She agreed to do that?"

"Yes."

Antonio signed off his computer and stood up, walking around to where his brother was. "Good. The Vallerio Roadster is almost ready for rollout. I think we've finally come up with terms that both sides can live with."

"What did you give them?"

"A partial share in the profits from the roadster and a seat on our board. We will be getting a seat on their board as well."

"Did you find out what their anticipated revenue will come from in the next quarter?"

He'd asked around and the Vallerio family was playing this one very close to the chest, but near as he could tell they had filed for new patents and would be releasing an updated carburetor design. A more energy efficient one. "It has something to with engines."

"That's good. See if we can get the exclusive rights to use it on our production cars for the first year."

"I will. I haven't broached the subject with Nathalie yet."

"Why not? You spend a lot of time with her."

"How do you know that?"

"Do you honestly think that I wouldn't pay attention to what you are doing? There is a woman involved and I don't want you to fall like Marco did."

Antonio shook his head. "Dom, it's time you stopped worrying about the curse. I think that Marco did break it. He's still winning and he seems happy."

Dom ran his hand through his hair and sighed. "I don't believe it. We haven't launched the new roadster and until it is successfully launched, we can't afford to take chances."

Antonio clapped his brother on the shoulder. As the oldest, Dom bore more responsibility than any of them. He was the one that *Nono* had groomed for the CEO position from the time they were old enough to talk.

"We will make this work. I can promise you that."

Dom nodded. "Some days just seem longer than others."

"I hear you," Antonio said. "I've been traveling too much. I'm ready to get everything taken care of so I can start loafing around again."

"You have never spent a day loafing in your life."

Antonio had to laugh at that. "Of course I haven't, but it does sound good."

"Indeed," Dom said.

Antonio looked at his older brother. They were workaholics, both of them, and he feared sometimes that if he didn't grab on to Nathalie with both hands, he was going to end up alone. Not that there was anything wrong with living a solitary life, but now that he'd a glimpse of what life could be, he wanted more.

"Do you ever wonder if we should have just followed Papa's path?" Antonio asked.

Dom turned and looked at him, studied him really, and Antonio regretted his words. Dom probably never doubted himself, and hinting that he, Antonio, doubted himself wasn't going over well.

"Never mind."

"No, I can't just dismiss this. If you are thinking along these lines, it can only mean one thing," Dom said.

Antonio shook his head. "It doesn't mean anything. Seeing Marco and Virginia together just made me curious."

Dom narrowed his eyes. "I was curious once, Tony, and I got burned. I didn't need a curse to harden my heart. I did it myself when I realized just how vulnerable a man can be to a woman. And most women can use that to their advantage."

Antonio knew that Dom's ex-lover had betrayed him in the worst way and that his brother would never risk his heart again. But he thought of Nathalie and the burgeoning feelings he had for her. They included trust, he thought.

He already trusted her and even if he never said the words out loud, he knew he loved her.

"I know I suggested romancing Nathalie Vallerio, but has that turned into something more?"

Antonio looked at his brother, straight in the eye, and told the biggest lie he ever had. "No, Dom. It's nothing more than an affair."

Nathalie backed away from Antonio's office almost running to get away from what she'd just heard. She refused to cry, but somehow her eyes didn't get the memo and tears burned the back of her eyes. She blinked rapidly trying to keep them from falling. She made it to the elevator and then had to stop.

She pressed the call button.

What was she going to do? She had taken back to her family the deal that she and Antonio had worked out. She'd compromised on things, believing that he was dealing with her fairly and that he was going to stand up and be the man she'd fallen in love with.

She should have remembered the lesson her great-aunt had learned the hard way…that Moretti men had only one true love and that was Moretti Motors.

She sniffed and blinked some more, but the tears were pooling in the corners of her eyes. She had no tissue to wipe them away. She never cried. She just wasn't the type of woman who would ever break down like this.

She heard the rumble of Antonio's voice and was horrified by the thought that he might catch her crying. She walked down the hall to the toilets on this floor.

She went inside and startled the woman already in there. She was clearly crying, her face red and splotchy. "Angelina?"

"*Ciao*, Nathalie. I'm sorry you've caught me this way."

It was funny but seeing the other woman's distress made her forget about her tears. At least for this moment. And that was all she needed. When she was alone she would deal with the heartache.

"Are you okay?"

"*Sì,*" Angelina said. "I wish I were one of those women who cried pretty."

Nathalie laughed. "Me too. Luckily I don't cry often."

"Unfortunately I do," Angelina said. There was an aura of sadness around her today.

"Do you want to talk?" Nathalie asked.

Angelina shook her head. "Not unless you know some way to keep from crying in front of others."

Nathalie thought about something her sister had read in a psychology journal a few years ago. To be honest she didn't believe it worked, but it always made her and Genevieve laugh when they mentioned it and laughter was a great mask for sadness.

"I did hear something, though I've never tried it," Nathalie said. "Don't laugh but if you tighten your buttocks, it's supposed to make you stop crying."

"And start laughing?"

"Well, it always has that affect on my sister and me."

Angelina laughed and then took a deep breath. "*Grazie,* Nathalie."

"You're welcome."

Angelina left the bathroom and Nathalie stood in

front of the mirror, trying to hold on to the laughter she'd shared with the other woman. She pushed her emotions down deep inside and tried to bury them, but it was hard for her to do.

She'd never been this vulnerable to a man before. And she didn't like that. She didn't like the fact that Antonio Moretti had done this to her.

She remembered what they had said in the beginning and realized she couldn't really get mad at him. She'd agreed that all was fair in love and war. It didn't matter that the circumstances of their relationship had changed for her. They'd laid down the ground rules at the beginning of their negotiations.

She was the one who had forgotten them. It was a mistake she couldn't afford to make again.

Breathing deeply, she left the ladies' room with a confident stride. Walking down the hall to Antonio's office, she practiced what she'd say, how she'd pretend that everything was normal until she got out of here.

She debated leaving now, not seeing him again. But he was expecting her and she had to use the new knowledge she had to her advantage. Something she wouldn't be able to accomplish if she left now.

Antonio's secretary, Carla, was at her desk this time when Nathalie came into the office.

"Is Antonio ready for me?" she asked after exchanging greetings.

"*Sì*, go on in."

The moment she pushed the door open and stepped into his office she knew this was a mistake. When Antonio turned to face her from the far side of his office and smiled at her, she wanted nothing but to confront him.

To demand he tell her to her face that she meant nothing more to him than a little affair to make the negotiations easier.

But she bit her tongue. She channeled her anger into a need for vengeance. Or at least that was what she told herself. Inside she realized that she'd trade vengeance for one more night in his arms.

Antonio was still distracted from his conversation with Dom. He wanted to get away from Moretti Motors and forget about his family for a little while. That was the past and Nathalie was his future. He didn't know how but he was going to convince Dom that there was no harm in falling in love.

He had spent a lot of time the last two weeks trying to make sense of everything, and having Nathalie here with him now made him realize that if he couldn't find a balance between Moretti Motors and Nathalie… Well, he'd have to choose between them, and Nathalie offered him something the car company couldn't.

She offered him a life beyond work.

He walked over to her to kiss her, but she turned her head so that his lips grazed her cheek.

"Are you okay?"

"Yes. Just had a long flight from Paris and I don't feel that your office is the best place for kissing."

"The boardroom is more to your liking?" he asked, teasing her.

She flushed and he saw an expression cross her face that he couldn't identify. "I guess so."

"Did your family agree to the terms we worked out?" he asked. They'd both spent long hours trying to make sure that the deal was fair for both sides.

"We can talk about that later. I'm here for a date with my main man."

"That's right. Pleasure first and then business," he said, but he could tell that something wasn't right with Nathalie. She never talked like this and he wondered if she wasn't having doubts.

Doubts about the deal or about them? Or was she simply tired? It was Friday evening and he'd asked her to come to Milan because he was going to propose to her. He wanted to do it at the house on Lake Como. He thought returning to the place where they'd first made love would be a nice touch.

In fact he'd planned for them to have cocktails and hors d'oeuvres in the boardroom first. "Will you come with me to the boardroom first?"

"Why?"

"I have planned a surprise for you, *cara mia.*"

He escorted her out of his office, glancing over at Carla. She nodded to him, letting him know she'd set up everything as he'd asked her to.

When he opened the door of the boardroom he saw flowers on the sideboard, a champagne bucket at the end of the table with a tray of food. And most importantly a slim gift-wrapped box as well.

"After you," he said.

She entered the room and then stopped. He stepped in behind her and locked the door so they wouldn't be disturbed.

"What is this?"

"Just a little predate."

"Antonio," she said, "you didn't have to do all of this."

"Yes, I did," he said. "Have a seat while I pour the champagne."

He held out one of the chairs for her and she slowly came to sit down. He put his hands on her shoulders and leaned over her to kiss her. This time she didn't turn away, but he noticed she was blinking a lot. "Is this okay?"

"Yes," she said, her voice a bit husky.

"Open this while I pour the champagne."

He handed her the box. He hoped she liked the

strand of Mikimoto pearls he'd gotten her. The creamy color of the pearls would look exquisite against her skin.

She held the box in her hands and stared up at him. "Why all of this?"

"To celebrate. Now that we aren't adversaries in the boardroom anymore, we can concentrate on our relationship. I see this day as a new start between us, *cara mia.* Open your gift."

She opened it slowly and he heard her breath catch as she stared down at the ocean-inspired strand of pearls. The pearls were offset by blue sapphires.

"This is beautiful."

"It is nothing compared to your beauty," he said.

He reached around her and took the pearls from the box. "Lift you hair up."

She did as he said and he fastened the necklace around her neck, bending to drop a kiss underneath the white gold clasp. She put one hand at the base of her throat where the pearls rested. He turned the chair around so he could see her eyes.

A sheen of tears glistened there and he knew this was a moment he'd remember all of his life. Having Nathalie here with him made him feel he'd been given the keys to the kingdom. And it was a kingdom he'd never thought to belong in.

That was what he wanted from her love, he

thought, what he needed from it. This acceptance and the desire to be with this woman for the rest of his life.

He knew that their marriage and engagement would not be easy, but he had a strong feeling that they could make it work.

He tipped her head back and kissed her, trying to show her with his mouth all the emotions he felt, all the words he couldn't say.

She parted her lips for him, her tongue thrusting past the barrier of his teeth. Her hands wound around his neck, drawing him closer to her.

He leaned in, put his arms around her waist and lifted her out of the chair and spun around so that he could lean against the table and hold her in his arms.

She pulled back and he saw something in her eyes he'd never seen before. He wasn't sure what emotion it was, but he knew it wasn't love.

"What is it, Nathalie?"

"I'm just trying to figure out something."

"What?"

"Are you giving me this gift as a thank-you for what I did to help Moretti Motors with the Vallerio Roadster? Or…"

"Or?"

"As a sop for your conscience since you romanced me around to your way of thinking?"

Eleven

"I didn't give you this for either reason. These are engagement gifts."

"There are more?" she asked, so afraid to believe what this man was telling her.

"Yes. I want you to be my wife, Nathalie. It has nothing to do with Moretti Motors."

"Really?" she asked.

"*Sì*. Sit down here. Listen to me. Over the past six weeks while we have argued and talked and become lovers, I've come to realize how much you mean to me. How much I need you in my life."

"How much?" she asked again. It was odd. She

should feel like crying now, but instead she felt oddly detached. It was almost as if she were watching the events unfold instead of actually participating in them. "Enough to give up the Vallerio name on the new roadster?"

"Why are you asking me that? You know that our affair has nothing to do with business."

She stood up and paced away from him. "No, Antonio. I don't know that."

"What is going on here?" he asked.

"I heard you talking to Dom earlier. I heard you tell him that I was just a romance."

"Merda."

"Cursing won't change the facts. And all of this is so lovely, but really it is over-the-top for the kind of affair you and I have…at least according to you."

"Nathalie—"

"Don't. Don't try to explain it to me, Antonio. I can't do this. I thought I could have it all. A man who cared for me…really cared about me and my family's respect, but I can see now I was wrong."

"What do you mean? The Vallerio and Moretti deal is done, just waiting for signatures," he said, walking over to her. He took her shoulders in his hands. "And our relationship is just starting. I couldn't tell Dom what I have only just figured out myself."

"What is that?"

"That you mean more to me than any woman ever has before."

He let his hands fall to his sides and she knew he was telling the truth. She did mean more to him than another woman, but for her that wasn't going to be enough. She wanted to be the love of his life. She wanted him to be enamored of her the way Gio was with Philomena. And that wasn't ever going to happen.

She could tell from the moment he mentioned marriage that he wasn't talking about a love affair and she knew that was what it would take for her not to grow bitter.

"That's not enough for me, Antonio," she said.

"Why not? We are both new to this relationship stuff. Give me time to get better at it."

She shook her head. "I can't."

"I don't understand, Nathalie. I have everything here that a woman could want. I will give you every-thing you need."

"Will you?"

"If it is within my power, it is yours," he said.

She wondered if she was being too hasty. Maybe she had misunderstood what he'd said to Dom. This boardroom certainly made it seem that way.

"What if I said all I really need is your love?" she asked quietly.

She felt the air go out of the room, as Antonio

stared at her. In that instant she had her answer and the tears started to roll down her face. She didn't try to stop them, knew that asking a man for his love and getting silence wasn't something that tricks could combat. She reached up behind her neck and took off the pearls and put them on the table.

"I think that answers my question," she said, walking to the door.

"No, dammit, it does not," he said.

"Yes, it does. Because without love, all of this is hollow. You'd think a man who grew up surrounded by the real thing would know the difference."

"You'd think a woman who spent her entire adult life in the business world would know a good deal when she sees it."

"I want more than a good deal from the man who asks me to marry him."

"I didn't mean that," he said.

"What did you mean, then?" she asked.

He raked a hand through his hair. "I don't know."

"What do you feel for me, Antonio? Is it only lust?"

He shook his head. "It is so much more than that."

"That's something at least. I think I made a mistake by starting an affair with you while we were adversaries."

"No, we didn't make a mistake. You and I we were drawn together from the very first."

"That doesn't mean we were meant to marry," she said. "We both wanted to win and I guess in the end I gave in because— Well, the why doesn't matter anymore…but I almost gave in on some important points for Vallerio Incorporated."

"Are you backing out of the deal we brokered because I can't say that I love you?"

He made her feel small and petty when he said it that way. "No. I'm backing out because we decided we don't need the money we'd make from the roadster."

"Fine. Walk away from the deal if that's what you feel you must do. But remind your board of directors that I treated you fairly and it's only your wounded pride that has you running back to Paris."

She had no rebuttal for him. She just unlocked the boardroom door and walked away as quickly as she could. She didn't want to think that she was using pride to protect her broken heart. To be fair, nothing could protect her broken heart. The pain there was already too intense for her to control.

Antonio glanced around the now empty boardroom. He had no idea how things had gone so wrong. Granted he had never proposed to a woman before, but he wasn't sure that he could screw it up that badly.

"What happened in here?" Dom asked from the doorway.

"Nothing. I...I had some— I asked Nathalie to marry me."

"What? I thought— Never mind that, are you okay?" He stepped into the boardroom.

"Yes, Dom. I know what you are thinking. I had it all under control this afternoon and now I'm afraid I may have messed everything up."

"The deal with Vallerio Incorporated on use of their name?"

"Yes. But more importantly my relationship with Nathalie."

"Which is more important to you?" Dom asked.

For once Antonio didn't stop to think about what answer his brother would want to hear. Instead he spoke the truth. "Nathalie is. And I let her go, Dom."

"You had to. You know that Moretti men don't make good husbands."

"How do we know that? Dad's happy and so is Marco."

"Yes, but they aren't cut from the same cloth as we are. We crave success the same way *Nono* did. What are you going to do? Would you choose Nathalie over Moretti Motors?"

Antonio thought about it. There was no way that he could pick between the two of them. And suddenly he realized he didn't have to. Without Nathalie in his life he didn't care if Moretti Motors was successful. "I can't choose."

"Then that's your answer," Dom said.

"What is?"

"You love her."

"I know I do. I was hoping that by not saying those words out loud I would be able to protect us from the curse. I'm sorry, Dom."

Dom shook his head. "I'm sorry, Tony, sorry that you feel like you have to apologize for falling in love. I was wrong to put you in that position."

"You might not feel like apologizing when I tell you that she's probably going to convince her board not to accept any deal with us."

Dom shrugged. "If that's what she has to do and if that's what you have to agree to in order to prove you love her, then we will find another way."

For the first time since everything went awry with Nathalie, he felt a ray of hope. "Yes, we will."

"I guess this means the curse is still in affect," Dom said.

"How do you figure?" Antonio asked.

"Well, if she's going to take the rights to the name…"

Antonio thought about it for a minute. "You know, I don't believe that's what the curse was about. I think the real curse is the fact that we would deny ourselves love to make the company successful."

"Really?"

Antonio shrugged. "I don't know for you, but for me I think that is the answer."

"What are you going to do?"

"Figure out a way to win Nathalie back."

Two weeks later Nathalie was back in Milan. Her sister and parents and the entire board of directors of Vallerio Inc. were in attendance as well. They'd taken the company jet and Nathalie was so ready to be alone by the time they got off the plane. She was tired.

Tired of sleepless nights and countless recriminations about the last time she spoke to Antonio. She'd tried to get out of this meeting, but Moretti Motors flatout refused to talk to anyone else from Vallerio. And so now they were all here for a big announcement from Moretti Motors. Something that demanded every one of them attend.

She'd tried to find out what was going on, but no one would share any details. Even Genevieve, who normally couldn't be shut up, just sat quietly next to her.

She had confessed to her sister that things had gone wrong with Antonio, but hadn't been able to tell her that she'd let him break her heart. She was a

sadder but wiser woman when she entered the
Moretti Motors building with her family.

Angelina greeted them all. "If you would all
follow me to the garden. We have a special presentation before we go up to the boardroom."

"What presentation?" Nathalie asked.

"That's fine," Emile said, preempting her. "We
will give you the time you need for the presentation."

"We will?"

"Oui, ma fille."

She shook her head and followed the rest of her
family through the building and out into the courtyard. In the center of the courtyard was a canvas-
draped car. She suspected it was the Vallerio
Roadster coupe, though she doubted seeing the car
would convince her board to go for the deal that
Moretti had offered. But she'd have to wait and see.

There were several seats in the courtyard and
Angelina directed them all to sit down. "Signore
Moretti will be right with you."

"Merci," Emile said.

Nathalie found herself sitting between her father
and her sister, tired and heartsick. Sitting here in this
garden, she remembered the first time she'd been here
and how it had been the start of her affair with Antonio.

She had hoped that her anger would be enough to

inure her to the love she'd felt for him, but it wasn't. And it saddened her to think that a man could use her and she'd still love him, but there it was—the truth of the matter.

"Thank you for joining us today," Dom said, stepping out of the factory and walking toward them. "I know that we have yet to reach an agreement for the use of Pierre-Henri's name on our legendary roadster and that very fact might be on your minds, but my brother has something very important he must do before we can go back to the boardroom."

She noticed that Philomena, Gio, Marco, Virginia and little Enzo were standing behind Dom. Why were they here?

Dom came over to her. "Will you come with me?"

She shook her head. "Why?"

"To make up for the trouble I caused," Dom said.

"What trouble?"

"Making my brother believe that he couldn't have the woman he loves and not disappoint me."

Woman he loved? Did that mean Antonio loved her? She stood up, putting her hand in Dom's. "Where to?"

"Right here," he said, leading her to the center of the courtyard right next to the canvas-covered car.

"Nathalie."

She turned to see Antonio striding toward her.

"Thank you, everyone, for coming today and for allowing me to do this in front of you," he said, speaking to their assembled families.

"As you are aware, our families have some misunderstandings between us. And because of that we haven't always communicated well with each other. I allowed that to ruin something precious to me."

Antonio turned to her. "I allowed the past to have more power over me than it should. I love you, Nathalie Vallerio. And I don't want to live without you."

"Antonio—"

"Shh. Let me finish, *cara mia.*"

He dropped down on one knee in front of her. "Please do me the honor of being my wife."

She stared down at him for a long moment and then drew him up to his feet. "Did you mean it when you said you loved me?"

"More than anything else in this world."

"What if my family won't agree to letting you use the Vallerio name?"

"That is why I'm asking you to marry me now. There is nothing that can change my desire to have you as my wife," he said, drawing her into his arms.

Nathalie looked at Antonio. She wanted to believe that he was sincere, but how could she be sure this wasn't the Moretti charm? The same charm that

Lorenzo had used on Anna. Was she simply being fooled because…because it was what she wanted to hear so badly? She realized she wanted Antonio's love. Not because it would end a family feud but because her life was so much better with Antonio in it.

She knew then if she was going to be happy for the rest of her days she needed Antonio and his love.

She hugged him tightly to her. "Yes. Yes, I will marry you."

Her family congratulated her and everyone agreed to go to the Moretti family home in San Giuliano Milanese after the meeting to celebrate.

They went into the boardroom and after a lot of haggling, Moretti Motors had the rights to use the Vallerio name on their roadster. They also got the rights to the new engine that her father had designed.

Everyone seemed happy with the way things worked out and when they went downstairs after the meeting, Emile and Gio both placed a temporary nameplate on the Vallerio Roadster. To see the sons of two men who fought and had grown to hate each other standing side by side felt right to Nathalie.

She hoped that with the bitterness of the feud in the past, both of their families would go on to much greater things.

"Are you happy?" Antonio asked, holding her

hand in his as they walked through the gardens at his parents' house.

"Happier than I ever thought I could be," she said. "What made you change your mind?"

"Nothing," he said.

She pulled away. "Nothing? Antonio, are you doing this on a whim?"

He pulled her back into his arms and kissed her. There was so much passion in that embrace that she knew without a doubt he loved her.

"I knew I loved you before you walked out. I had thought that confessing my love would doom it, but then I realized that by hiding it I was cursing us to a life without each other."

"Are you sure you love me?" she asked, unable to believe she was really going to get to spend the rest of her life with Antonio.

"Positive, *cara mia*. And I'm going to make sure you never doubt it or me again."

"How will you do that?" she asked, though she already felt his love surrounding her.

"By telling you of my love often, by paying attention to the little things that make you happy, by making you feel like the center of my world, because that is what you are."

"And what will I do for you?"

"You've already done it. You brought color to my life and made me realize that business wasn't the only thing I could live for." And he kissed her to seal the deal.

* * * * *

*Don't miss the thrilling finale of
Katherine Garbera's
Moretti's Legacy miniseries,
THE MORETTI ARRANGEMENT
On sale May 12, 2009, from Silhouette Desire*

*Celebrate 60 years of pure reading pleasure
with Harlequin®!*

*Step back in time and enjoy a sneak preview of an
exciting anthology from Harlequin® Historical
with*
THE DIAMONDS OF WELBOURNE MANOR

This compelling anthology features three stories about the outrageous Fitzmanning sisters. Meet Annalise, who is never at a loss for words… But that can change with an unexpected encounter in the forest.

Available May 2009 from Harlequin® Historical.

"I'm the illegitimate daughter of notoriously scandalous parents, Mr. Milford. Candidates for my hand are unlikely to be lining up at the gates."

"Don't be so quick to discount your charms, my dear. Or the charm of your substantial dowry. Or even your brothers' influence. There are as many reasons to marry as there are marriages."

Annalise snorted. "Oh, yes. Perhaps I shall marry for dynastic reasons, or perhaps for property or influence. After all, a loveless, practical marriage worked out so well for my mother."

"Well, you've routed me on that one. I can think of no suitable rejoinder." Ned rose to his feet and extended his hand. "And since that is the case, let me be the first to wish you a long and happy spinsterhood."

Her mouth gaped open. And then she laughed.

And he froze.

This was the first time, Ned realized. The first time he'd seen her eyes light up and her mouth curl. The first time he'd witnessed her features melded together in glorious accord to produce exquisite beauty.

Unbelievable what a change came over her face. Unheard of what effect her throaty, rasping laughter had on his body. It pounded a beat upon his ear, quickly taken up by his pulse. It echoed through him, finally residing in his stirring nether regions.

So easily she did it, awakened these sensations within him—without any apparent effort at all. And she had called him potentially dangerous? Clearly the intelligent thing for him to do would be to steer clear, to leave her to the tender ministrations of Lord Peter Blackthorne.

"You were right." She smiled up at him as she took his hand and climbed to her feet. "I do feel better."

Ah, well. When had he ever chosen the intelligent path?

He did not relinquish her hand. He used it to pull her in, close enough that he could feel the warmth of her. "At the risk of repeating Lord Peter's mistake and anticipating too much—may I ask if you'll be my partner in battledore tomorrow?"

Her smiled dimmed. Her breath came a little faster. His own had gone shallow, as if he'd just run a race—and lost. He ran his gaze over the appealing lift of her brow and the curious angle of her chin. His index finger twitched.

"I should like that," she said.

His finger trembled again and he lifted it, traced the pink and tender shell of her ear, the unique sweep of her jaw. Her pulse leaped beneath her skin, triggering his own. Slowly he tilted her chin up, waiting for her to object, to step back, to slap his hand away.

She did none of those eminently sensible things. Which left him free to do the entirely impractical thing.

Baby soft, the skin of her lips. Her whole body trembled when he touched her there.

He leaned in. Her eyes closed, even as she stood straight against him, strung as tight as a bow. He pressed his mouth to hers. It was a soft kiss, sweet and chaste. And yet he was hot and hard and as ready as he'd ever been in his life.

She drew back a little. Sighed. Their breath mingled a moment before she slowly backed away.

"Oh," she breathed. Her dark eyes were full of wonder and something that looked like fear. He took a step toward her, but she only shook her head. His outstretched hand fell to his side as she turned to disappear into the wood. This was the first time, Ned realized. The first time, since he'd come to the house party at Welbourne Manor, that he'd seen her eyes light up.

* * * * *

Follow Ned and Annalise's story in May 2009 in
THE DIAMONDS OF WELBOURNE MANOR
Available May 2009 from Harlequin® Historical

Available in the series romance section,
or in the historical romance section,
wherever books are sold.

**We'll be spotlighting a different series
every month throughout 2009
to celebrate our 60th anniversary.**

Look for Harlequin® Historical in May!

Celebrations begin with
a sumptuous Regency house party!

Join three scandalous sisters in

THE DIAMONDS OF
WELBOURNE MANOR

Glittering, scintillating, sensual fun
by Diane Gaston, Deb Marlowe
and Amanda McCabe.

**60 years of Harlequin,
600 years of romance
in Harlequin Historical!**

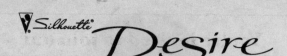

You're invited to join our Tell Harlequin Reader Panel!

By joining our new reader panel you will:

- Receive Harlequin® books—they are FREE and yours to keep with no obligation to purchase anything!
- Participate in fun online surveys
- Exchange opinions and ideas with women just like you
- Have a say in our new book ideas and help us publish the best in women's fiction

In addition, you will have a chance to win great prizes and receive special gifts! See Web site for details. Some conditions apply. Space is limited.

To join, visit us at

www.TellHarlequin.com.

REQUEST YOUR FREE BOOKS!

2 FREE NOVELS
PLUS 2
FREE GIFTS!

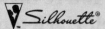

Passionate, Powerful, Provocative!

SDES09

Harlequin® Historical
Historical Romantic Adventure!

If you enjoyed reading
Joanne Rock in the
Harlequin® Blaze™ series,
look for her new book
from Harlequin® Historical!

THE KNIGHT'S RETURN
Joanne Rock

Missing more than his memory,
Hugh de Montagne sets out to find his
true identity. When he lands in a small
Irish kingdom and finds a new liege in the
Irish king, his hands are full with his new
assignment: guarding the king's beautiful,
exiled daughter. Sorcha has had her heart
broken by a knight in the past. Will she be
able to open her heart to love again?

Available April
wherever books are sold.

Silhouette *Desire*

COMING NEXT MONTH
Available May 12, 2009

#1939 BILLIONAIRE EXTRAORDINAIRE—Leanne Banks
Man of the Month
Determined to get revenge on his enemy, he convinces his buttoned-up new assistant to give him the information he needs—by getting her to *un*button a few things....

#1940 PROPOSITIONED INTO A FOREIGN AFFAIR—Catherine Mann
The Hudsons of Beverly Hills
A fling in France with a Hollywood starlet turns into a calculated affair in L.A. But is she really the only woman sharing his bed?

#1941 MONTANA MISTRESS—Sara Orwig
Stetsons & CEOs
It's an offer she finds hard to refuse: he'll buy her family's hotel—*if* she'll be his mistress for a month.

#1942 THE ONCE AND FUTURE PRINCE—Olivia Gates
The Castaldini Crown
There is only one woman who can convince this prince to take the throne. And there is only one way he'll ever agree—by reigniting their steamy love affair.

#1943 THE MORETTI ARRANGEMENT—Katherine Garbera
Moretti's Legacy
When he discovers his assistant has been selling company secrets, he decides to keep a closer eye on her...clothing optional!

#1944 THE TYCOON'S REBEL BRIDE—Maya Banks
The Anetakis Tycoons
She arrives in town determined to get her man at any cost. But suddenly it isn't clear anymore who is seducing whom....

SDCNMBPA0409